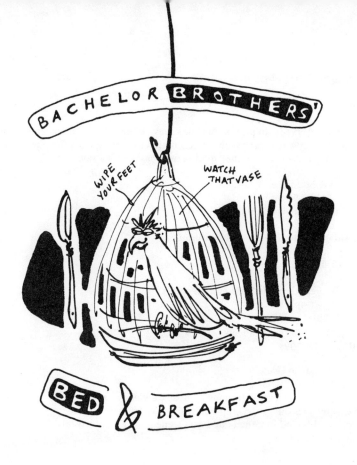

BACHELOR BROTHERS'

WIPE YOUR FEET

WATCH THAT VASE

BED & BREAKFAST

BILL Richardson

Douglas & McIntyre
Vancouver/Toronto

Douglas & McIntyre
1615 Venables Street
Vancouver, British Columbia V5L 2H1

Canadian Cataloguing in Publication Data

Richardson, Bill, 1955–

 Bachelor brothers' bed and breakfast
 ISBN 1-55054-112-9
 I. Title.
PS8585.I353B3 1993 C813'.54 C93-091630-1
PR9199.3.R53B 1993

Editing by Saeko Usukawa
Design by Rose Cowles
Front and back cover illustrations by Rose Cowles
Typeset by Vancouver Desktop Publishing Centre
Printed and bound in Canada by Best Gagné Book Manufacturers, Inc.
Printed on acid-free paper ∞

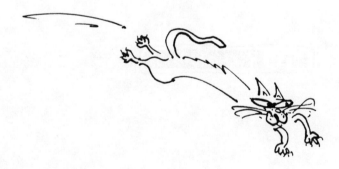

To my parents,
and to those who are found
where there is said to be nobody,
this book is fondly dedicated

Contents

"**B** is for bachelors,
and the wonderful dinners they pull out of their cupboards
with such dining room aplomb and kitchen chaos."

M. F. K. Fisher, *An Alphabet for Gourmets*

Getting There

If you get there, it will be in your own time and way. I discovered the Bachelor Brothers' Bed and Breakfast when I was in a terribly distracted state of mind. It was a season in hell, the worst of times, a winter of discontent. Work had soured, love had taken a Greyhound out of town, the days were empty husks. I was bereft of purpose. Oh, it was bleak, bleak, bleak. One day, I put myself in the car and simply drove. I had no idea where I was going or why. I had no intention when I left my home of getting on a ferry and going to an island, no intention of meandering around its back roads, no notion that I would wind up, at dusk, in a lost little valley, turning up the driveway of the Bachelor Brothers' Bed and Breakfast. Had I known any of that, I would surely have packed along my copy of *Moby Dick*.

Is there a literate person anywhere in the world who doesn't have a list of books he or she Must Read? If there is, you can call me Ishmael. I have such a list, and *Moby Dick* is on it.

I do own a copy of *Moby Dick*. I bought it years ago, in a nice Penguin paperback version. It has every appearance of being a book that is well loved and often referred to. This is because I drag it along with me every time I go on vacation or out of town on business. It has been carted from city to city, country to country, and beach to beach. It has been on planes and boats and trains. It is dotted with sunscreen and pasta sauce. The pages are dog-eared and worn. The spine is cracked. Anyone picking up the damn thing would think that its owner could recite the whole text by heart. But the truth is that I know nothing about *Moby Dick*, save that it has something to do with a whale, who may or may not be white. I believe there is also a missing limb, that may or may not be a leg.

I don't mean to be obtuse about this. Whenever I set out on a trip, always with this great classic in tow, I have it in my head that I will find the time to read it; or to at least make a beginning. But inevitably, I give in to distractions. Snorkelling. Bar hopping. Looking for love in all the wrong places.

The only way I will ever make my way through this nautical saga is to go somewhere where reading will not be a possible distraction or subsidiary activity but the entire thrust of my excursion. Ironically, one of the few times I ventured forth without *Moby Dick* was the occasion I stumbled on a place where such a vacation would have been possible: the Bachelor Brothers' Bed and Breakfast.

The brothers who own and operate this B & B, which is located on one of the islands that populate the Strait of Georgia, between Vancouver Island and the mainland, are named Hector and Virgil. They are twins, now in their fifties. As you may have surmised by the name of the enterprise, they are bachelors. They inherited their house, as well as an income, from their mother. Untroubled by the odious necessity of working but possessed by humanitarian instincts, they decided to open their doors to the public as a refuge, a retreat, a haven for bibliophiles.

It was a natural impulse. Both brothers are avid, lifelong readers. They share the oppression felt by the gentle, sometimes confused people who are their paying guests; people who see that the ratio of books available to time available is terribly skewed. Hector and Virgil think of their B & B as a way of redressing that dreadful imbalance; a way of offering readers the chance to finally revel in *Silas Marner* or *À la recherche du temps perdu* or *Persuasion*.

Guests at the Bachelor Brothers' Bed and Breakfast are provided with comfortable, simple accommodations. Most bring their own reading material, although everyone is invited to use the brothers' library, which is very substantial. Visitors are provided with breakfast—eggs, sausage, bacon, toast, fruit, muffins—and given access to the kitchen between the hours of noon and 7 P.M. to prepare their own lunches and dinners. This rather peculiar arrangement, which I have never seen elsewhere, fosters a happy sense of communality that nicely compliments the more solitary, introspective business of reading.

I now feel privileged to call Hector and Virgil my friends, although it is a friendship that has developed by way of letters rather than through personal contact. Circumstances have not allowed me to return to their island since my first come-by-chance visit. I hope to do so one day soon, *Moby Dick* in hand. However, I was sufficiently intrigued by what I found there that I persuaded Hector and Virgil to write a series of dispatches about their B & B for CBC Radio, where I have the good fortune to work. The brothers agreed to their broadcast and to this publication on the condition that neither their surname nor the exact location of their home be revealed. Their business operates now to capacity, and they have no need to bolster it further through advertising.

An unusual feature of Hector and Virgil's B & B is their guest book, which is in fact a large scrapbooklike album they call "Brief Lives," after Aubrey. Their guests are encouraged to write their own stories in it, brief biographical sketches. There are now over a dozen volumes of "Brief Lives." I am grateful to the brothers for making a selection of these pieces and for editing them in order to shield identities and protect privacy.

There are those who think that the Bachelor Brothers' Bed and Breakfast is simply a hallucination, or a fiction of my own devising. Let me say to all those doubting Virginias that, yes, there really is a Bachelor Brothers' Bed and Breakfast. It is a treasure and, like most treasures, hard to discover. But it is well worth the effort. When you find it, you will know it. And if you have adventures getting there, it will be all the more worthwhile.

A Little Bit More About Us

My brother Hector and I are twins, although you wouldn't know it to look at us. We are fraternal rather than identical. There are a few superficial resemblances. We are both tall. We share the family nose and chin. Otherwise, we are quite dissimilar. Hector is more conventionally handsome. He has kept most of his hair. And his face is less lined than mine, which I attribute to several factors. In the first place, I am older. By almost twenty minutes. As well, Hector is constitutionally happy; and I don't discount the effect of his long association with Altona Winkler. Altona sells a line of cosmetic products, and Hector has had unfettered access to a great many moisturizers.

We were raised by our mother, a pioneer in the art of single parenting. Most people hearing our names suppose her to have been a classicist. This is not the case. We owe our historically resonant monikers to nothing more glorious than a bizarre coincidence that erupted on the morning we first sucked air. That very day in May, under the sign of Taurus, twin bulls were born at a farm not far from here. The event was accorded a banner headline in the *Occasional Rumor*, our local newspaper. There was a charming human-interest angle to the story. It seemed the farmer who oversaw the delivery had for years been courting the school's Latin teacher. He named the new arrivals Hector and Virgil in her honour. She was so touched by this that she finally agreed to throw in her lot with his.

Mother, of course, felt a kind of pressing urgency around the business of attaching names to her offspring. She was surprised, in those days before ultrasound, to find herself saddled with two babies rather than the one she had been anticipating. She read the story of the bulls when she was still in a state of mild shock and, I suppose, alarm. It would have been hard enough to settle on one name, let alone two. And so it was—in her groggy, achy, postnatal condition—that she decided Hector and Virgil would suit us just as well as any of the other available handles.

That was over half a century ago. We have lived in our house, in this valley, on this island, all our lives. That we have never pulled anchor and moved on always engenders wide-eyed wonderment in strangers and first-time guests.

"How unusual! How very old world!" they exclaim. No doubt there have been many armchair psychologists who have analysed the defects of spirit that have kept us rooted here and prevented us from marrying, spawning, and leading lives that are altogether more normal.

I accommodate these speculations. I am tolerant of them. We both understand that we are anomalies in the annals of late twentieth-century sociology. I am too settled in my ways and too secure in my thinking to try to excuse the way we live. And I can offer no explanation, except to say that time went by. One day we looked around, and this is what we had. It is fine. We are happy to be here.

By now, I have lived here for so long, and have such a deep connection to this sod, that I can divine stories from the earth around me, like a dowser can find water. In quiet moments like this one, when I close my eyes, I can see so clearly how it happened. I feel it, even: the shuddering of earth that shook this island and its neighbours loose from the mainland, scattering them like dice. I imagine how some sensible glacier, migrating south, dragged its ponderous feet along and carved out this valley and made these hills. It must have paused a geological moment too long on the western flank of the valley; for whereas the hills to the north, south, and east are smooth and round, the west is capped by a wide flat ridge.

It is to this slight plateau, from which one has the most beautiful and commanding view of the valley, that I have come to write these few words. The January sky is oyster-coloured and striated by the smoke from many chimneys. One of them is ours. Hector is burning the dross of the festive season just passed. This is our time of year for a general house cleaning, when we take a respite from tending to the needs of guests and apply ourselves to some of the maintenance tasks that are part and parcel of running a busy bed and breakfast. It is at a moment like this, when I get a rare chance to relax, that I realize how consuming and taxing a business it is. But joyful, I hasten to add.

We have had a light dusting of snow, which is unusual in these parts. Bravely setting aside the hemorrhoidal fears that come so easily to men of my age, I have swept off a bench and am perched upon the chill planks, enjoying a soft and enveloping quiet. I sit among those whose enduring occupation is the respecting of silence; for this is the site our distant forefathers chose for the cemetery. I imagine they thought that planting those who had been reduced to worm fodder in a place with a beautiful vista was a sign of respect: which indeed it is. Today, this land would almost certainly be snapped up by some real estate mogul and developed. Happily, we retain a sufficiently atavistic attitude towards the placement of remains that a graveyard, once it is established, is rarely disturbed. I think it unlikely, at least in my lifetime, that anyone will come along and suggest that the community would be better served if this tranquil and sacred space were transformed into an "adult community" or a townhouse complex called "Elysian Estates." But one never knows. This sacrosant turf was once before buffeted by change.

As we are neither populous nor short-lived, there hasn't been a tremendous rush to occupy the many deep and narrow lots that are available for suitable tenants. About twenty years ago, our civic bright lights determined that a portion of the grounds could be tastefully transformed into something more overtly parklike. They cast their minds about for a scheme that would preserve the solemnity of the surroundings, yet make the place more welcoming for the local living.

Village meetings were held. Opinions were solicited. Petitions were circulated. Schoolchildren wrote essays. In the end, it was decreed that the cemetery would share the flat hilltop with a golf course.

This announcement was not greeted with unalloyed enthusiasm.

The bandstand lobby cried foul. The English garden contingent huffed. But the village council, which at the time was dominated by men who were seeking some agreeable pastime for their middle years, stood firm. When it came time for the deed to be done, no one lay down in front of the bulldozers: except for those whom longstanding immobility had robbed of the option of rising.

On the day of the grand opening, one golfer had a heart attack and perished while trying to extricate his ball from a sandtrap. Some people said this proved the golf course was an abomination. Others saw it as evidence that the two facilities could mix and mingle. Time passed, and the whole fracas petered out. Now, it is simply an arrangement we live with, the golf course and the cemetery blending together in a harmony of pocked symmetry. There is no fence, hedge, or other line of demarcation to indicate where a hole in one ends and one in a hole begins. It's a good arrangement for the sports-minded dead and for athletes with a philosophical bent. "*Carpe diem*," they can be heard to mutter, before their calls of "Fore!" ricochet from hill to hill and out across the valley.

Our recent snow, though slight, has proved a sufficient deterrent to keep even the most fervent golfer from venturing out. This is fine with me. It means there is no chance a rogue projectile will bounce off an angel or praying Virgin and do me irreparable brain damage. When I look about at the various epitaphs, many of which are dreadful, I think that it might be wise for me to plan my own summation. I have considered:

> Virgil lies beneath this stone,
> A bachelor, content alone.

No. I think not. Perhaps:

> Virgil lies here, gone to seed,
> Time enough at last to read
> Nestled quiet in his nook,
> Time aplenty, but no book.

No. Too ribald by half. When all that remains of me is a morsel of doggerel scratched in marble, I want something that will be representative and balanced. Happily, I feel no particular pressure to decide on a final script.

Looking around the cemetery at the various memorials and mausoleums, you can read a sort of pocket history of these hereabouts. The industrious winds and rains have made the etching on the earliest stone barely discernible.

Anthea Swystun
1848–1869

There are no other facts of her short life and passing. Still, we who are native to this out-of-the-way place feel a sense of kinship with her. Anthea is part of local lore. Her story has been feelingly told and retold, an oral heirloom. We all grew up knowing that Anthea had been unable to withstand the awful rigours of childbirth. Nor was her child inclined to linger. Known only as Baby Swystun, his small marker is beside his mother's: not even a proper headstone, but a pretty rock that looks like a gnarled tooth.

It is a simple grave, but mythic nonetheless. Anthea's role in the pageant of our history and the weather-worn evidence of her short time on earth have taken on a certain totemistic power. It has been a tradition for succeeding generations of women "in the family way" to come here and pay her their respects, to touch the snaggled stones, and to ask their long-dead sister for her assistance during their impending travail. Even our mother—an immensely practical and clear-minded individual who pooh-poohed any kind of superstition—made her pilgrimage when she was encumbered with the squirming lumps that would become Hector and me. However, she refused to let some poor pale shade take any credit when we both of us erupted into the world, one after the other, with the easy speed of circus performers blasting out of a cannon.

"I don't know why everyone makes such a fuss about it," she would say when, as little ones, we would ask to hear the story of our arrival. "I could have balanced my chequebook at the same time!"

Mother was perfect, and like most perfect people she was vastly irritating. She was efficient in all things: living, birthing, working, dying. She lived hale and hearty for seventy-four years, enduring no illness more severe than a very occasional head cold. She could hear a leaf burst from its bud on a tree outside, had all her teeth, and a great many opinions. She was a fine plumber. She could diagnose an automotive problem at a single glance. She never slept for longer than five hours, except on the occasion her dependable heart turned traitor and she never rose again.

She was an atheist and a freethinker. In compliance with her wishes, we kept her ashes in a ziplock bag in the freezer, attending the day we could incorporate them into a household project. Eventually, we mixed her up with some cement we used to repair a bit of cracked garden paving. She would have snorted derisively to see us inscribe her dates in the tacky concrete and would have been amused to note that the numerals were smudged by our cat, Waffle, when she tromped across our handiwork directly we had gone inside.

A crow has just settled in the elm tree behind me: a harbinger of who knows what. Time to move on. The light is fading, in any case, and I have miles to go before I sleep. I would like to practise the bassoon. It is my night to cook dinner. And I will certainly find that there remain a great many chores to tend to before we open the doors to our guests.

So I will make my way out of here, and home. I will stop by the grave of Anthea Swystun before I leave. I'll touch her stone and make a wish for the new year. I'll ask for the usual blessings. For luck. For peace. For fortune. For us, and for you, too. ♦

Helen

Another sojourn at the Bachelor Brothers' Bed and Breakfast: my seventh January visit. What better place to come to steady the nerves for the year ahead? I return home with my usual reluctance. Back to the flesh-eating cold of the prairie winter! It's been so funny to hear you go on about your few flakes of snow. We won't have weather this mild in Winnipeg until April. May, even. But June makes it worthwhile.

Ever since I was a little girl, I've lived for June. The soft time of year. When June came, the whole world sighed with relief. Then, not even the most freakish weather would bring snow. The two rivers that run through the city, and regularly flooded it, signed a truce with their banks: they wouldn't challenge them for another year. The lawns shed their winter dinginess and had a short green heyday, before the sun and hot wind scorched them brown. The elm trees that arched over our street turned the colour of mint. There were lilacs. Purple and white. The air was sweet with their breathing. The time of the singing of birds had come.

We grew up slowly back then. My granddaughter, just ten, knows about safe sex. She plays so much Nintendo she has the reflexes of a fighter pilot. She tells me she hates dolls, though I think she still might play with them in her private moments. There are dances at her school, and she has already asked a boy on a date! She falls in love, and with an intensity that astonishes me. Her mother assures me that she is typical. But I despair for her and for her friends. They are being forced into growing like hothouse flowers.

My childhood was so different! On my fourteenth birthday (June 17, another reason I looked forward to that month), my parents arranged for half a dozen girlfriends and me to go on an early evening hayride. Afterwards, we joined other neighbourhood children in a game of hide-and-seek. We had cake and cocoa (or possibly Ovaltine). And then we were allowed to camp out in a big canvas tent my father had pitched in our back yard.

We talked quietly into the night, planning our lives, confessing our small crushes, giggling into our hands. Around three in the morning, we crept from the tent and went for a walk around the neighbourhood in our nightgowns. We shone a flashlight on the darkened houses. We picked some snapdragons from the next-door widow's garden. We felt full of evil. Then we returned to the tent and slept deeply.

I spent my summers reading. Once or twice a week, I took the streetcar to the William St. Library and came home with great armloads of books. I was completely indiscriminate. Anything would do. Jane Austen. The Brontës. *Gone with the Wind. The Red Badge of Courage.* Books on self-improvement. "How-to" books. Alone in my room, I would lie on my bed, or sit in a rocker in front of the open, south-facing-window—the hot wind blowing across my face—and plough through. Page after page, book after book. I was just passing the time, waiting, waiting, waiting for I didn't know what. For something to happen.

Some books I returned to again and again. I was—am—especially fond of Robert Louis Stevenson. Even *A Child's Garden of Verses* I still read; and not with nostalgia. I love those poems! In September, in 1939, when I was eighteen and studying secretarial and accounting skills at business college, I left a library copy of *Treasure Island* on the streetcar. My borrower's card, with my name and address, was inside. That night, a young man appeared unannounced at the door. I was in my room, practising for a typing speed test. My mother called from downstairs.

"Helen! You have a visitor!"

What must she have thought? Certainly, she couldn't have been more surprised than me when I walked into the living room and saw him, this tall, gangly boy, all limbs and freckles, seated in an armchair and talking to my father. He was my very first gentleman caller.

"How do you do I found your book," he said, all in a nervous rush, pushing it at me with both hands.

"I'll leave you two young people to talk," said my father, rather gracelessly; or so I thought at the time. He liked to tease me about the absence of beaus in my life. This chance visit must have pleased him no end!

A clumsy silence. I had no idea what to say, or how to act. I shielded myself with formality.

"It was very kind of you to return my book, Mr. —"

"Hawkins. Jim Hawkins."

I must have gaped.

"Jim Hawkins? But that's the boy in *Treasure Island!*"

"Don't I know it," he said and laughed.

I began to laugh, too.

And as the whole weight of coincidence and strangeness settled on us, we laughed and laughed and laughed until we were quite literally weak in the knees and had to sit down.

Something had been shaken loose. Now there was nothing between us. We sat and we talked. My mother brought us tea and cookies. He stayed longer and we talked. About what? I can't recall, exactly. I just remember that we spoke with great freedom and abandon. I had never had this kind of easy and immediate communion before; would never have expected to have it with a man. We must have talked about our lives, our families, our notions of the world. We certainly discussed the war, which had just started, and where he expected to go. We talked until my mother appeared again in the living room, to say that it was almost eleven and that if I expected to do well on my test in the morning, I should go to bed.

That was how it started. Jim Hawkins kept calling. He came to see me when he had a day leave from the army training camp. And in January, the day before he got on the train for Montreal, we were married. Nothing was turning out as I'd imagined it. I had envisioned a June wedding: my favourite month, a temperate day, the smell of lilac everywhere. But this was Winnipeg in January. The drifts were six feet high, and you could hardly see through the air, it was so full of frost. The church was freezing, and we both wore our coats. Only our families and one or two friends were with us. The news was as bleak as the weather. All you could smell was danger.

All that night we held each other and talked. Jim slept, finally. I never did. I lay beside him, staring into the dark. I could see nothing but the future, and it was to be so happy! Whatever my gifts, prophecy is not among them. I never saw him again. He was never numbered among the known fallen. He was consigned to the limbo land of the missing, about whom the worst is presumed. For a while, I had vivid imaginings. Gradually, they left me.

It's a commonplace story. A thousand other women my age can tell it. I married again, right after the war. It was a June wedding. The church was full. I had my babies. Now they have theirs. I still love my husband. We still live in Winnipeg. We are fit and active. We belong to a club that walks, all winter long, miles and miles through shopping malls. In February, we go to Palm Springs. We have a timeshare there. But every January, I come here, by myself. My husband understands. I read *Treasure Island*. I think about Jim, about how for a few years I shared his name. I remember who we were, and the wonder of that time. I smile. I haven't cried for him for years.

Thank you again! And thanks most particularly to Waffle, who has brought me both a mouse and a shrew. ☗

The Coming and Staying of Waffle and Mrs. Rochester

I can't remember who said: "I don't like writing. I prefer to have written." I understand this, absolutely. I can always find something I'd rather do than write. Tonight I meant to get to it straight away. Instead, I changed the shelf liners and went through the fridge looking at all the "best before" dates, just in case there was something that had expired. Good thing, too. There was a bottle of Italian dressing that was three weeks past its prime. Who knows what damage it might have done, if left to stay?

I was just about to sit at the kitchen table with pen and notepad, when the three retired librarians who are staying with us—all reading Barbara Pym and A. S. Byatt—challenged me to a round of Scrabble. Poor things! They had no way of knowing they were dealing with a merciless barracuda, with a keen eye for the triple word score. They never stood a chance. They trooped off to their rooms looking rather wilted, as though the wind had been taken out of their buns.

So now I am flushed with victory and too agitated to sleep. Although it is nearly midnight, I have settled down to the business of writing, here in the kitchen. I have my two favourite food groups nearby: a tin of Poppycock and a bottle of sherry. Virgil padded through a few minutes ago for his bedtime glass of milk.

"Now is the time for all good men to take to their beds and read Hardy," he muttered as he headed off to his room with a copy of *Jude the Obscure* under his arm and our cat, Waffle, on his head. His posture was exemplary.

Remember how in the Old Possum poems, Mr. Eliot wrote about the challenges of naming cats? Our pretty calico chose her own name on the very day she chose us. She arrived a few months after our mother's death, and just around the time we were thinking about opening the house as a B & B.

This has never been a grand inn. We strive for simplicity in all things. We are not like those luxurious bed and breakfasts you read about in *Gourmet* magazine: where guests descend in the morning to find a groaning board stacked with golden pancakes and steam trays spilling over with sausages, bacon, and ham; boxes and boxes of cold cereal all arranged in their ranks; mangoes and melons and papayas pared and sliced and arranged in starlike clusters on silver trays, and fresh-squeezed orange juice in crystal decanters.

We offer conventionally prepared eggs. We deal with the usual meat products in the usual ways. We provide muffins, fruit, coffee, and toast with the expected assembly of condiments. That's all.

At the very outset, before we had settled on our "less is more" philosophy, we thought we might try something grander. On the day the cat came, we had spent a happy morning rummaging in the attic, taking an inventory of serviceable linens and hunting down flatware: the bits and pieces we'd need when the business got rolling. Of course, we kept on unearthing oddments that required exclaiming over: photographs, toys of childhood, and so on. What particularly caught our attention was our mother's old waffle iron.

It was a Proustian moment. In an instant, we were sucked back down the funnel of time, to that long-ago season when waffles were our mother's passion. We could see her so clearly, beaming with pleasure as she set them on the table, with their crusty ridges and their absorbent valleys. They were miracles of fearless symmetry. For her, it was just a passing culinary fancy. But it made a lasting impression on her sons.

I looked at Virgil. Virgil looked at me. We read each other's minds. We would serve our guests waffles for breakfast! Of course, we would need to hone our skills. And that very afternoon we set out to do just that: to transmute base batter into gold.

Historians annoy me with their blinkered selectivity. They took the time to write down the names of those who invented the telephone, the atom bomb, and the cotton gin. But the geniuses who left us with that truly worthwhile legacy of recipes have gone unheralded. Why don't we know the name of the person—and I would wager it was a woman—who came up with the idea of the waffle? To take flour, eggs, and milk, which on the surface seem to have nothing to say to one another, and to combine them; then to pour the stuff onto a scorching griddle; and to finally look at the result, cock an ear to the heavens, and know that it must go by the euphonious name of waffle: well, it boggles the mind!

This is what I was thinking as we prepared to wake the sleeping iron. Virgil fixed the batter. I slathered the hardware with oil, so that its pock-marked children would have an easy release. I held my hand close above it, while Virgil stood at the ready with his thick elixir. At the moment I felt my palm might combust, I shouted out, "Now! Pour it now!"

Just then, a cat leapt through the open kitchen window onto the counter and deposited a very large mouse, or maybe a small rat, exactly on the spot the batter was meant to go. I don't know if the prey was alive or dead at the time of delivery. I let loose a loud and not very manly trill of alarm, and slammed the lid of the iron down on the ill-starred rodent. It is for situations like this that we coined the word "unpleasant."

Looking back, it seems extraordinary that the cat was able to maintain such agility in an advanced state of gravidity. When we returned from taking the waffle iron to the trash, she had taken over the bread box and was giving birth to seven pretty kittens. Each of these found a happy home. The mother, duly christened Waffle, remained with us. And very sweet she has proved to be, too, especially since we arranged with our veterinarian to have her "altered." I understand this is the preferred term amongst those in the know. I would rather call a spay a spay.

Guests who make their way here for the first time must always be warned that there is a cat on the premises. The air is thick with allergens, and Waffle is extremely peremptory insofar as laps are concerned. Any vacant abdomen in a state of repose is fair game. However, we have noted that a passion for books and a fondness for cats are very often points of intersection on the ven diagram of personality.

Our other resident pet, and the one who really rules the roost, is Mrs. Rochester. She was our mother's parrot. In fact, she is still her parrot, even though Mother has been dead all these years. Parrots tend to bond to one person, and Mrs. Rochester is no exception to the rule. The petty intrusion of mortality has not diminished their connection.

Mrs. Rochester is a yellow-fronted Amazon (*Amazona ochrocephala ochrocephala*). She is full of days. She has been part of our domestic scene for as long as I can remember. Like Waffle, she appeared mysteriously and unbidden. In fact, she too came into the house through an open window. She flew into the attic and sat on a sewing mannequin. She shrieked and carried on, like the poor mad thing for whom she was named.

This happened a few weeks after we were born. Our mother, of course, hurried to see what was making the racket. Mrs. Rochester took one look at her and fell in love. She left the mannequin, settled on mother's shoulder, and gave her a playful nip on the ear. It was the beginning of a long friendship.

Parrots are unusual in these parts even now. Then, they were entirely unheard of. But no one answered Mother's enquiries. No one indicated that they had had such a bird and lost it. Mrs. Rochester simply came. She stayed. And she remains with us still. In many ways she was more a nanny than a pet. She was uncanny in her ability to sputter out at appropriate moments such warnings as, "Watch that vase!" or "Go to your room!"

She still says these things. But like the grandfather clock that stopped short never to go again, she has steadfastly refused to add to her lexicon since our mother passed on.

Unlike Virgil, I have very little interest in things psychic and am not much of a believer in mediumship. But there are times when I think our mother uses Mrs. Rochester to speak to us or our guests.

"Wipe your feet!" she bellowed at the librarians earlier today when they came in from a walk with rather wet and grimy looking tennis shoes.

"Don't do it!" she commanded this evening during the Scrabble game, when the most skilled of my opponents was about to bring out all her heavy guns and spell the word she thought would take her over the top and to victory.

"Be quiet, Mother!" I hissed, much to my embarrassment and to the surprise of our guests; for offering unsolicited advice about Scrabble or bridge, or any one of the other games at which she was expert, was just the kind of thing Mother loved to do. Luckily, the librarian just couldn't pass up the chance to spell out "excoriate." By simply tagging it with an "S," I left them all in the dust.

Mrs. Rochester slept in her mistress's room. The shock of finding Mother dead in bed was almost eclipsed by hearing her parrot bellow the last phrase she had deigned to learn: "Fuck off!" She had never said this before. Unfortunately, it has become one of her favourite oaths.

How did she pick up such a vile expression? I can only conclude that these were Mother's last words. She was a spirited creature. I imagine that she reared up in her bed, like an angry mare, and roared it at the reaper when he entered without knocking.

Good grief! The time! Now it is well and truly late. Fatigue has found me. The Poppycock's done, and so is the sherry. Time to say amen. At last, I have written. ⌂

Alice

I am very glad that you have Waffle in residence. It makes me feel at home. I have three cats myself, and it is a wrench to leave them, even though I know they are well looked after by my great niece, Monica. Monica is a librarian, too; but so very different from me or from any of the librarians of my generation. Times change, so what could be less surprising? Her hair is short and glistens with gel. She cultivates a kind of wrinkled look that would never have passed muster when I was starting out in the profession. But then, her options are much broader than mine ever were. Monica prefers not to work with the public. Instead, she has a high-paying job with some huge firm of accountants. She has told me what she does, and it sounds exquisitely dull. It has everything to do with computers and nothing to do with books. To each her own. She seems happy enough. She gets six weeks of vacation a year and likes to go to women's music festivals. I don't ask too many questions.

Two of my cats are Persians. They are twin brothers, just like you. They look like bath mats and have the disposition of pit bulls. Their names are Osbert and Sitwell. Their companion is a big orange tom named General Levine, after the piano piece by Debussy. We live in Mississauga in a condominium I bought a while back. Until I moved there, I couldn't even name six major appliances. My nephew Andrew said it was a smart investment. I just think it's a nice place to live.

I was with the public library for over thirty years. I've been retired for ten, but find that I make much the same use of my time as I did when I was working. I read. I see my friends for movies and plays and lunch. I travel when I can afford to. And I write poetry. Here is a little verse that was inspired by Waffle. She is a splendid cat and has an admirable way of appearing out of nowhere when someone is about to sit down with a book. I think that anyone who has ever tried to read when there is a cat in the room will be able to identify with it.

> They say that cats are fickle things,
> Impervious to laws:
> Except the rule that when one reads,
> They'll knead you with their claws.
> The reason that they need to knead's
> Instinctual perhaps.
> We only know for certain that

They hop into our laps
The moment that we lift a book,
Then splay upon our loins
And rake their nasty nails along
The stretch from knee to groin.
Each time you take a book in hand,
It's never known to fail,
They try to lie upon the page,
Manoeuvring their tails
So that they brush against one's lip:
They then assume a pose
That's positively yogic,
With their butts against one's nose.
And if you put them on the floor,
They carry on abominably;
The only way they're happy is
To know you well abdominally.
Oh kitty cat upon my lap,
You know I love you well;
Though why you have to read with me,
I simply cannot tell.
But love, I want my book in peace,
And so I'll risk your wrath,
By dumping you upon the floor
And reading in the bath.

It's not, I grant you, a prize-winning effort. But I hope you like it. I dedicate it to Waffle, and to bibliophilic kitties wherever they live. Thanks again for your warm hospitality. ⌂

Our Patrimony

The observant reader may have noted that while we have both talked about our matrilineal heritage, we have neither of us mentioned any paternal connection. And thereby hangs a tale. My brother Hector and I are part of that honourable if rather melodramatic league who can look wistfully into the distance, sigh, and say, "We never knew our father." Indeed, our mother met him only once.

When Mother was twenty-one, her parents packed her off to Paris to attend a finishing school. It was their intention that she should be instructed in the language, in the ways of refinement, and in the home manufacture of pastry. These skills would equip her to play the role in which they had cast her: socialite wife and helpmate to J. MacDonald Bellweather II, scion of J. MacDonald Bellweather I, founder and editor of our local newspaper, the *Occasional Rumor*.

However, no sooner was she out of the parental line of vision than Mother determined to chart her own course. On her first day in Paris, she fell in love with an auto mechanic called Jean-Marie, the godson of her landlady. Their meeting was the stuff of high romance. Directly upon entering her *pension* room, she ran to the window and threw open the shutters so that she might gaze on the narrow streets, three storeys below. She had no way of knowing that Jean-Marie was straddling a ladder outside, dutifully painting those very shutters, a Sunday chore he had undertaken as a favour to his godmother. He was knocked precipitously from his perch and fell to the cobbles beneath. Mother, properly alarmed, rushed to his aid. She cradled his head in her lap and muttered the few words she had learned from her phrase book:

"Avez-vous des timbres? Voulez-vous du sucre?"

Jean-Marie, only slightly concussed from his fall, was wildly smitten with the pretty young woman who was his assailant one minute and his nurse the next, and who whispered such charming nonsense. Mother, too, was greatly taken with her victim. He was installed in the room next to hers, and all that afternoon she sat by him, cooing sweet nothings and applying cold compresses to his head. They were young. Their bodies were gymkhanas for dancing, coltish hormones. And before long, she had moved from bedside to bed.

Mother knew a good thing when she found it. For the next six weeks, rather than schooling herself in the intricacies of the imperfect subjunctive and *comme il faut* methods for making *choux* pastry, she hung around with Jean-Marie. She went with him every day to the garage where he worked and watched while he performed automotive surgery. She acquired an impressive repertoire of Gallic invectives and an ability to disassemble, repair, and reconfigure an engine.

Of course, it couldn't go on. Eventually, her parents learned from the principal of the finishing school that their daughter was an incorrigible truant; and there was a pleading letter in tortured English from the owner of the *pension*, begging them to intercede, for Jean-Marie was after all engaged to a nice French Catholic girl called Cecile. There was an angry volley of telegrams. The foreign service was called into action. And Mother, wrested from the arms of her lover, found herself on a boat bound for Montreal.

Her parents' chief concern on her return, once they were satisfied that their child's indiscretions were not going to take on any visible consequences, was that the Bellweather family not learn of her spoilage. They watched her like a hawk for any signs of miscreant behaviour. And they forbade her to have anything to do with automobile repair, for which she had both a passion and a gift.

On a hot August afternoon, six weeks before she and J. MacDonald Bellweather II were meant to forge their lasting bond, an itinerant bookseller, who peddled his wares from the back of his truck, passed through our valley. He stopped in front of the house where Hector and I are now pleased to live. My mother saw him from the

21

porch, where she was swinging prettily, with her ankles crossed, on the glider. Her watchful guardians, dulled by the sun and worn out with vigilance, dozed in deck chairs on either side. She rose quietly and crossed the lawn to see if the bookish higgler might have something that would help her lift the miasma of depression that had hung over her since her forced return.

She browsed through the selection, rejecting wholesale his suggestion that she might like a little Dickens.

"Or possibly something by Willa Cather?"

"I don't have time for fiction," she said. "I can only suppose the people who read it must have terribly dull lives."

"Well," said the merchant of words, "if fiction isn't the ticket, perhaps you'd like to have this collection of picture post-card views of the City of Light."

Mother leafed through the volume of Paris photos. On every page she saw a landmark or street that brought the image of the lost Jean-Marie to her mind and the sting of shameful tears to her eyes.

"Yes," she answered, choking back a sob, "I think these will do very nicely."

She turned on her heel and headed back to the house, clutching her new book to her breast, unaware that a tiny part of her, a uterine Ulysses, was making his way into port, where shortly he would wreak considerable havoc. She heard the door of the truck slam, heard the engine cough and wheeze like something out of Thomas Mann. She turned and watched, fascinated by the consumptive sputterings that grew evermore faint, until the thing heaved and died.

On the porch, her parents slept in their chairs, a two-headed Cerberus snoring before the gates of hell. She set down her album and marched back to the truck. You can imagine how surprised the bookseller must have been when the young woman who only minutes before had stood before him all distraught returned with a new sense of purpose, rolled up her sleeves, and wrenched open the hood of his lifeless vehicle. Unsatisfied with what she saw therein, she asked for his jack, elevated the chassis to a suitable height, and slid beneath.

He was too astonished to protest her unsolicited ministrations and was without the competence to offer any real assistance. He could only stand back and watch, feeling the faint stirrings of desire for this pretty girl, whose skirt was hiked up over her knees and whose face, when she re-emerged, was grease-streaked.

"I've found the problem. Come and look."

He joined her on the pavement. And that is where it happened. In front of the house where my brother Hector and I have subsequently lived our whole lives long, while our grandparents snoozed in their chairs on the wide expanse of porch; beneath a broken-down old truck full of books, we were conceived.

She must have been moved to consummate her short-term relationship with our father there and then by a combination of factors: nostalgia, the erotically associative smell of grease, and the availability of a man who seemed happy to comply with her wishes. Mother used to say that if there is any space in the world that can accommodate two human bodies, in either the vertical or the horizontal position, and if there is sufficient room for some minimal manoeuvring, then that space has been used for lovemaking. Anyone who questioned this would be treated to the story of her oily thrashings.

When they were done, she completed the repairs, slid out from beneath the truck, and with a curt wave goodbye, tiptoed past the guardians of her tattered virtue and went straight to the bathroom where she washed away the grimy outward evidence of her activities. The man who planted the seed that would make him our father drove off in his newly healed truck, over the hills and far away.

This all happened six weeks before the long-planned wedding, a wedding for which no expense had been spared. At the rehearsal on the evening before the nuptials, with all the bridesmaids and attendants and ushers looking on, Mother announced that she was in the family way and that she felt J. MacDonald Bellweather II should know her pregnancy was the result of a random encounter with a travelling salesman whose name she did not know.

"And we did it under his truck," she added, driving the knife point home.

What wouldn't I have given to a have been a fly on the wall at that moment! Mother used to relish telling us the story of what happened next. She made it sound like something out of Aeschylus. It was one of our favourite bedtime stories.

"You'd have thought I'd confessed to a murder," she said, while tucking us in and tousling our hair.

We hung on her every word as she described how, for a few moments, a charged and electric silence hummed in the air: an enormous icicle that hung on the cusp of falling.

Her father broke the short-lived, uneasy quiet.

"Under a truck?" he asked, in a strangulated voice. They were the last words he ever spoke to her.

"What will the neighbours think?" was all her mother could manage, before fainting dead away.

The matron of honour and most of the bridesmaids and ushers followed suit. The few left standing had no idea what to do. They simply went to stand alone in corners, trembling.

The Bellweathers beat a hasty retreat to the kitchen, where they held a family conference and determined that it would not be in the best interests of J. MacDonald II to claim these damaged goods as his own. They said a curt farewell to our grandfather, who sat in his chair with his gaze fixed on the middle distance. They nodded good day to our grandmother, who lay prone on the floor. They stepped over the various bodies and left without acknowledging or offering to assist our mother. She moved calmly about the room, administering smelling salts in an effort to revive the fallen.

One by one they came to and staggered outside, gasping for air. One by one they filled their pockets with pinwheel sandwiches or slices of date square and walked out into the darkening evening, awestruck at the news that had been laid before them. By the time our grandmother had been helped up the stairs to bed, the telephone lines that were only then beginning to crisscross our little valley were red hot.

This is a very small community. Memories are long. It will not surprise anyone to learn that our growing up was marked by the whispery residue of scandal.

"Her poor parents!"

"And then when she had twins!"

"The shock almost killed them!"

It was true that the two old people did not choose to live long after our advent. I recall my grandfather only slightly: a remote figure who seemed never to stir from his chair, as if he had been frozen alive on the afternoon he learned of our imminent arrival. My grandmother, who withered on the stalk very shortly after our birth, I don't remember at all. I believe she spent her declining days wandering neurasthenically about the house, rousing herself every so often to call down curses on my mother or to revile herself for ever having children.

A few weeks after our double-barrelled emergence into the world, we began to receive in the post the packages that would constitute our patrimony. Once a month or every six weeks, Mother would find in the mail another gift of books. From one year to the next they came. At first there were picture books. Then came collections of fairy tales. Next there were illustrated children's classics: *Crusoe*, with pictures by N. C. Wyeth; and the just published *Winnie the Pooh*, with the lovely Shepard drawings. As we grew older, there were *Boys' Own Annuals*, and tales of derring-do: *Biggles Versus the Swastika*, and seafaring tales by Charles Marryat. There were anthologies of poetry and various collected works: Tennyson, Browning, Yeats. There were plays by J. M. Barrie and George Bernard Shaw, novels by the Brontës, Fielding, Hardy, even D. H. Lawrence. The postmark was never the same: Saskatchewan. Montana. North Dakota. Nova Scotia. There was never a return address. Never a covering letter. But there was never any doubt as to their source.

To her credit, Mother preserved even the earliest of these unsolicited offerings carefully, until we were of an age to enjoy them and to understand their significance. She never made any comment when they arrived, other than to say, "Your father again." She simply passed them on to us with a slightly disapproving look. Her disapprobation was due not to their source but to their content. Poetry. Plays. Fiction. She always felt that reading should be more practical than pleasurable. *Jane's Guide to Aircraft Carriers* was on her bedside table the night she died.

"It's your father coming through in you," she'd say, when she saw us absorbed in a novel. It was as though we were some kind of palimpset, and she regretted or resented the evidence of his authorship. I think it stirred up the waters of her controlling nature to be reminded that she was not the only lifeguard of our gene pool.

There are mysteries here. Is it possible that even a predilection for fiction can live in the cell? If so, does free will stand a chance? And what moved this man, this itinerant bookseller whose name we've never known, to insinuate himself into our lives in this odd and generous way? How did he even know that his brief stop in our little valley, on that hot August afternoon in 193—, was not without consequence?

Perhaps none of it matters so very much. What is, is. I will always be grateful to him: not just for playing his cameo role in coaxing us into being but for the early provision of so many imagined worlds.

When we were sixteen, the books stopped coming. Who can say why? I have thought of every scenario. What is certain is that by that time, the damage was done. We were addicts, hooked on books, on their reading and on their acquisition. And so we became who we are: gentle and bookish and ever so slightly confused. It is not a bad way to be, when all is said and done. Which, for the moment, it is. ♠

The Top Ten Authors Over Ten Years
at the Bachelor Brothers' B & B

Margaret Atwood

At almost any given time, you can count on finding at least one of our visitors reading something by Margaret Atwood: poetry, criticism, short fiction, novels. Her wit, which can be caustic, and her world view, which some call bleak and others call realistic, always provoke discussion. We have noted that men often feel hard done by and overly tarred by her brush. Women, on the other hand, generally think she is spot on. Never the twain.

A. S. Byatt

When we first opened our doors as a bed and breakfast where gentle folk might come to read, a very occasional discriminating soul would arrive with *The Virgin in the Garden* and, later on, *Still-life*. But for the most part, any discussion of the name A. S. Byatt engendered the question, "Who's he?" However, the publication of *Possession* changed all that. On at least two occasions, every one of our guests has arrived with Mrs. Byatt's long and clever novel about academic grave pillaging tucked beneath an arm. "Did you read all the poetry?" they ask one another, in a guilty, conspiratorial way. Those who skipped over Mrs. Byatt's Browning-esque versifying and hurried on to the narrative can take comfort in knowing they are in the clear majority.

Robertson Davies

The bearded *éminence grise* of Canadian letters is thoroughly acclimatized to the hoary heights of the best-seller lists. A Jungian and convinced Trinitarian, Mr. Davies is forever turning out wry and psychologically insightful novels in clusters of three. We would remind readers not to neglect the first of his trilogies: the Salterton books. *Leaven of Malice* (1952) is among the funniest novels ever written in Canada.

Michael Ondaatje

That Canadian writers are so well represented on this "top ten" list seems to us a quiet testimony to both the excellence of our domestic product and to the discerning ways of our clientele. Michael Ondaatje's prize-winning novels, his poetry, and his evocative memoir *Running in the Family*, are increasingly among the books plumbed by our visitors. We use the word "plumb" advisedly. We keep a copy of his amusing chapbook, *Elimination Dance*, in each of our three bathrooms.

Marcel Proust

Bookcases the world over contain the first volume of Marcel Proust's lengthy and elegant sequence, *À la recherche du temps perdu*. Readers the world over pray to be visited by a mildly debilitating disease: something that will necessitate their confinement to a chaise in a cork-lined room; something that will drain them of all ambition, save the urge to get beyond the famous dipping of the madeleine that happens early on in *Swann's Way*. Many of our guests, plagued by persistent good health, choose to devote their time in our home to the reading of Proust. "Because it's there," they answer, when we ask them why. We have an honour roll on which we inscribe the names of those who actually make it through all thirteen volumes.

Barbara Pym

For many years, Barbara Pym had a small but loyal band of followers who would identify one another by drawing fish in the sand or through other arcane methods of symbology. Her quiet, rather sad novels about church-obsessed spinsters drew a wider cult after Philip Larkin identified her as one of the great neglected writers of our time. He was right. Now, she has the audience she deserves, and many of them are our guests.

Leo Tolstoy

See Proust. Neither of us has read *War and Peace*, but it is plainly one of those monuments of literature that cry out for tackling. That hernia-inducing tome is very often among the luggage of visitors to our home, and those who have waded through it swear by it. Virgil has read *Anna Karenina* and has not felt the same about trains since.

Anthony Trollope

Anthony Trollope owes his considerable popularity largely to television and the adaptations of the Palliser novels that turn up from time to time on the small screen. We would guess that fully 90 per cent of our clientele can hum the theme music to "Masterpiece Theatre."

Anne Tyler

The purpose of reading is not necessarily to have one's own world view confirmed or mirrored back. But it is nice when it happens. It is not difficult for either of us to imagine any number of Anne Tyler's confused and gentle characters turning up at our door. We rather suspect that many of our guests see themselves reflected in her pages and take a certain comfort in being validated through fiction. Who can blame them? It is a benign form of narcissism.

Virginia Woolf

What a remarkable cottage industry has sprung up around the life and writing of Virginia Woolf! It has endured for decades and shows no sign of abating. Our guests pack along her novels, her letters, her journals, and any number of biographies or critical studies. If some enterprising scholar were to assemble her collected grocery lists, they would find an eager audience. Little wonder. She was an elegant, daring stylist, possessed of a most vigorous mind. Many, many of our visitors have named their cats Virginia and Vanessa, Virginia and Leonard, Virginia and Vita, Virginia and Lytton. We wonder if she would have been pleased. ⬆

A Legacy of Eggcups

Being a guest—even a paying guest—can be tricky work, especially at a bed and breakfast. People choose a B & B because it's less impersonal than a hotel. There are nicer pictures on the walls. The lamps aren't bolted to the tables. But sensitive guests, such as we attract, frequently find it hard to adapt to being in someone else's house. Over and over we insist that they should "make themselves right to home!" Still, they treat the place with more than appropriate deference, tiptoeing here and there, speaking in whispers, exhaling with undue caution, apologizing if they sneeze.

"Don't you miss your privacy?" they often ask.

Nope. We enjoy our visitors. Both my brother and I feel the richer for the bits of the world they track in with them. Of course, it was an adjustment at first. For instance, having people around does mean that you have to maintain a semblance of decorum. You can't parade around the place starkers, displaying the gifts God gave you. Not that we were either of us much inclined to that sort of thing, anyway. Only one abandonment causes me pangs of regret. I've had to give up those occasional leisurely mornings when I would lounge in my bathrobe in the kitchen, swilling black coffee and smoking cigarettes.

Virgil, ever the big brother, laid down the law a week or so before we opened.

"Hector," he said, in the prim voice that is a sure sign of an impending lecture, "it's about the cigarettes. No doubt many of our guests will be sensitive to smoke. We should have a house rule that there be no smoking indoors. And that will mean you, first and foremost. Anyway, it's time you quit. No one smokes any more. Even Princess Margaret has given it up. And don't you think it's time you retired that bathrobe? It looks like it's been through the trenches."

"Doesn't Princess Margaret wear hers any more?" I asked. He ignored that. Virgil is usually quite contained; but when a Calvinist fit seizes him, he's impervious to tempering forces. Like sarcasm. As usual, though, he had a point. So I gave up cigarettes. And I only wear my bathrobe in the privacy of my own room.

I think many men have bathrobes like mine. They are the adult male equivalent of a security blanket: worn to a frazzle and held in place by several knotted neckties. Common sense or decency says "Throw it out." But emotion intervenes. These dressing gowns are like bread pans. They can be spot cleaned when necessary but should never be subjected to wholesale laundering. All but the worst and the stickiest of spills—tablespoons of jam, for instance—should be absorbed by the terrycloth, become part of an aromatic whole. Robes like this are statements of personal history. They are archives where the discerning eye or nose can distinguish the ghosts of breakfasts and bedtime snacks past.

This is the kind of garment you have to keep hidden from those who are keen of nose and quick with bleach. By all means, keep them out of the reach of dogs. I know this from embarrassing experience.

Just a few months back, I got up in the middle of the night to visit the bathroom. I put on the robe I have just described, feeling certain that there would be no one around to be offended by it, and padded down the hall. Halfway to my appointed destination, I became aware that I was dragging an unaccustomed weight behind me. I looked over my shoulder, and what to my wondering eye should appear but the little cocker spaniel who was visiting us in the company of some two-legged guests. Her jaws were fastened firmly around the hem. I tugged. She pulled back, with a fervour I wouldn't have thought possible in so small and seemingly genteel a pooch.

"Tut tut now," I cajoled, "let go. That's a good puppy."

She stared back at me. Her eyes were full of fierce territoriality. Plainly, she was past the point of verbal suasion. All at once, she gave a herculean pull. The neckties I use to hold it in place loosed their knots. The robe slipped from my shoulders. One more pull, and she had wrested it altogether from my body. There I was, naked in the hallway, chilled and very much awake. I watched with horror and fascination while Cookie—that was her name, believe it or not—charged off with this relic. I gave hot pursuit.

"Cookie!" I hissed, as she pelted down the hall, dragging her fetid prize. "Cookie!" I pleaded, like a truculent four-year-old begging for a snack. She headed downstairs. I followed on, trying to step on her drag and bring her to a halt. Round about the kitchen we chased, through the living room and breakfast room and library, waking up Mrs. Rochester.

"Fuck off!" she yelled.

We ran back upstairs.

"Cookie!" I called, quite loudly by now, forgetting about the guests who were sensibly asleep. Finally, she threw herself on the floor, in front of the door behind which her owners lay dreaming. At last, I had her cornered.

"Cookie," I seethed, grabbing hold of the robe. "Goddamn it, you little bitch! Gimme!"

I tugged and grunted. She tugged and snarled. I heard the door handle turn. This had a sobering effect. I leapt into the air, astonishing myself with my own agility, and flattened my body against the wall. This took some doing. My body is not as flat as it once was.

"Cookie," came the voice of one of her blessedly myopic owners, peering out into the gloom, "what are you doing? Why are you growling? And where did you get that filthy rag? Let it go, Cookie. Let it go. Good girl. We don't know where it's been, do we? Oh my! It does smell!"

She scooped up her pet, who was still whining after her trophy, and returned to bed.

31

"Doesn't smell so bad," I whispered, defensively. As I stood there in the hall, catching my breath and examining the robe for damage, Virgil came by, also bathroom bound. He simply arched an eyebrow and said,

> Oh what can ail thee, knight at arms,
> Alone and palely loitering?

It amazes me that he can remember his Keats when it's not even five in the morning.

A few years ago, I made a will. One of the provisions is that any of the parts of me that are useful at the time of my demise should be harvested for use by the living. Maybe I should also make some kind of provision for the bathrobe. It could be useful for students of forensic medicine. They could examine bits of it and try to determine the make-up of particular stains and blotches.

"Ah, yes. This seems to be the remnants of an egg. Soft boiled, I would say. And no later than 1978."

It would be a shame if the advancement of science were held up, simply because I didn't take the time to add a simple clause to my final testament.

Soft-boiled eggs and the perils of perishing intestate are pivotal features in one of our more tender family stories: that of second cousin Aloysius. As is the case with an alarming number of our relatives, we never had the pleasure of knowing him. But if clannish lore can be believed, Aloysius was a skirt-chasing, heavy-drinking, fast-talking ne'er-do-well. He came to Canada from England when he was in his late teens. Until he was well into his forties, he lived off the avails of gambling. His basic stake was an allowance sent to him by the Canadian agents of his mother's London solicitor. For over twenty-five years, she believed she was putting her son through a cowpunching school. We have a copy of one of his letters to her, in which he ascribes his delayed graduation to an overly tender heart that stayed his hand whenever it came time to wield the burning brand.

One morning, we are told, after a lascivious night in a stylish brothel on Ethelbert Street, in Winnipeg, Cousin Aloysius was invited to breakfast with the Madam. This, I guess, is like a favoured shipboard passenger being asked to the captain's table. The maid brought in soft-boiled eggs in cunningly painted porcelain cups. Each cup had a hinged lid, and the Madam's, when she opened it, played "Musetta's Waltz."

Aloysius was tough and jaded. He'd rather booze and carouse than look at a picture or a moving vista. But the eggcup moved him. Its gay tinkling touched him at some part of his soul that was so deep and remote it was unsullied by his chronic dissolution. Tears welled in his eyes and spilled onto his toast.

"Mais, vous pleurez, Milord!" exclaimed the tender-hearted Madam, who was native to St. Boniface. She offered on the spot to sell him the eggcup for a price that was a mere fraction of its sentimental value. Aloysius didn't hesitate for an instant. His billfold bulged with ill-gotten gains. He drew it out and turned the lot over to her. It was one of those on the road to Damascus experiences. In the twinkling of an eye, his life was changed.

He spent the rest of his days, and the rest of his income, travelling the world, seeking out musical eggcups. He picked them up in Istanbul and Paris, in Geneva and Beirut. According to the letters he sent his mother, he one day hoped to open a shop in Plymouth or Tunbridge Wells and sell them. But his obsession would never allow him to give them up. He wanted them for himself. He craved them, just as he had craved women and liquor. He would sit by himself, alone at night in his thin-walled room, and play the eggcups over and over again. One morning, he was found dead. Murdered, it appeared. Nothing had been taken. There was no clear motive. It was whispered that he had been done in by a consortium of irritated neighbours, pushed over the edge by the tintinnabular cacophony.

His collection numbered several hundred cups. He died without leaving a will, and as word of his demise spread throughout his former network of gamblers and free-lance brigands, creditors crawled out of the woodwork on two continents. Each had a thirst to slake, and most of Aloysius's treasures were sold at auction. The dispersal took several years. By the time the demands on the estate had been satisfied, our mother was his closest surviving relative. She fell heir to the dozen remaining eggcups: all that were left of Aloysius.

She had no interest in this kind of geegaw. She kept them in the attic. In time's due course, they fell to Virgil and me, along with the house where we were born and raised, and where we have lived all our adult lives. Why should we go? Who would want to, especially on those days we have a full complement of guests; when they open their eggcups, the breakfast room rings with "Voi Che Sapete" and "Love's Old Sweet Song" and "Believe Me If All Those Endearing Young Charms." It is magical.

When I look at what we have been given—this house, our books, and a dozen musical eggcups—it's clear that we are doing the work we are meant to do. What else could we be in the world but the proprietors of the Bachelor Brothers' Bed and Breakfast? This is not just a vocation. It's the working out of destiny. Happy, happy! And spring is on the verge. Soon, we will have a garden full of birds to bolster the chorus of eggcups. ⌂

Wendy

At least once a week, someone comes through the office with a card that needs signing. Neil is recovering from gall bladder surgery, or Brenda has had a baby. Heather is moving on, Judy's mother has passed away, George has been promoted, and all of them deserve some heartfelt, personalized message of congratulations or condolence.

This makes me so anxious. I can never think of anything to say! By the time the card comes to me, it's crisscrossed with good or worthwhile wishes. "Hey! Have a great trip! Don't give us a second thought!" "I'm thinking of you during this difficult time. Call if there's anything I can do."

I imagine the recipient opening the envelope and reading the witty or touching thoughts of colleagues. He laughs. She smiles, fondly. Then she sees "Cheers! Wendy." Or "Take care! Wendy." I imagine her scratching her head. "Wendy? Wendy who?"

Somehow, the simple act of signing a card feeds my every insecurity. I react to guest books in the same way. So, usually, I just ignore them or ask my husband to deal with it. But I decided to grit my teeth in this case, mostly just to tell you how much we appreciate finding a bed and breakfast where we can bring Cookie.

Cookie was not our idea. A few years back, we agreed to babysit her for our neighbours when they took a long trip to Europe. She was just past being a puppy and still very much given to learning about the world by means of her teeth. She chewed everything. Shoes, purses, the legs of furniture. She didn't discriminate. We would never have agreed to look after her had we understood how much work a dog is and how much damage they can do when they work solidly for an eight-hour shift.

Anyway, our neighbours were gone for three months, and during that time we pretty well weaned Cookie away from her chewing habits. She settled into the business of being a cute cocker spaniel. When the three months were up, I was feeling quite attached.

Our neighbours had not weathered Europe well at all. The trip, it seemed, had been an ill-conceived ploy to save their marriage. I suppose they got the dog for the same sad, stupid reason. Whatever the case, they had determined that directly they returned home, they would begin divorce proceedings. Could we keep Cookie until they had things settled?

I'm sure I don't need to fill in the blanks. Cookie remains with us, and I don't know how we ever managed without her. I said that to Glen the other day, and he said, "I feel that way about the fax machine." But he loves her as much as I do. Both Cookie and I see right through him. Especially on cold nights, when he coaxes her to sleep on his feet.

So thanks for letting us bring her along. I was happy to see how well she got along with Waffle and Mrs. Rochester. I suspect they must have taken her aside when we weren't looking and laid down the law.

Glen says thanks for not making him feel lowbrow for reading

Robert Ludlum and Len Deighton. He was a little taken aback to see so many of your guests reading Trollope. Me, I had a Dick Francis feeding frenzy. And I'm blissfully unrepentant. Take care! ♠

The Recovering Heart

A few years ago, two days after our forty-third birthday, I had a small heart attack. Attack is perhaps too harsh and percussive a word to describe the incident. It was more like a fret or a spat. A tussle. I only had to endure a couple of days in the hospital and felt quite well within a week. Nonetheless, it had the salutary effect of waking me up to my mortality. I sat myself down to make a list of everything I want to accomplish before time proves itself finite.

If I'd done this ten years before, it would have been a very long list indeed. Learn Russian or Mandarin. Study beekeeping. Become a naturopath. Travel to India. Build a log house. Get married. Be a better bridge player. Any of those would have been possible. The world seems so much more full of availabilities when we are in our thirties.

But when I actually sat at my little table (the same one I have used since I was a schoolboy) with my notebook and pen at the ready, I could think of only one looming ambition, other than honouring the ongoing social imperative of being a decent tenant on the planet. I wanted to learn the bassoon.

I love music and have always been an enthusiastic listener. But my practical skills are wanting. I do play the piano, badly, and have done so since I was a child. Like everyone else who grew up here-abouts (with the exception of Hector, who was exempted from lessons because of a tin ear that resisted every effort to tune it), I was tutored by the formidable Mrs. Dangle. She pronounced her name with a French lilt, "Dohngla," but the anglicized pronunciation suited her better. In fact, she could not have had a more apt handle, for everything about her suggested the pendulous. She had wattles and several chins that wobbled when she spoke, or bellowed, which she did more frequently. She had hugely fleshy forearms that swayed like half-furled sails when she demonstrated a run of arpeggios. About her neck she always wore a loopy garland of pearls (the last gift given her by the late Mr. Dangle) that arranged itself in double-helix patterns on the jutting overhang of her bosom. She chain smoked, but in order that her hands might be free to smack offending fingers, she simply left the cigarette dangling from her lips. The smoke curled up into her right eye, which teared and drooped.

Mrs. Dangle was a nasty bit of work. Still, I wanted to please her. And I was, by nature, predisposed to try. I was not one of those children who had to be chained to the bench with a derringer pointed at their head in order to practise. On the contrary, I couldn't wait to begin! I loved everything about it. I loved the bigness of our old "upright grand" with its gold scroll of name and the sight of its guts: hammers and strings. I loved the pleasing symmetry of the keys, the brush of my fingers against them, the immediacy of their response: a true and tuneful sound. I loved looking at the sheet music, and thinking about how something fleeting and insubstantial and emotive, like music, could be translated into something practical and concrete: lines and staves and black dots on sticks.

Unfortunately, and rather unfairly, all this fondness did me no good. I was shy on talent, and that was all there was to it. I was—am—encumbered with some kind of biblically inspired brain blockage that keeps the right hand from knowing what the left hand is doing. My eyes see the treble line and the bass line. They pass the information on to whatever part of the brain handles the decoding of such abstract messages. But the signal gets scrambled between there and the fingers. Oh, I can muddle through something slow and lugubrious by Satie or the middle movements of Clementi sonatinas. But as soon as the going gets tough, I cave in altogether.

Mrs. Dangle, who was not one to mince words, identified me as a musical mediocrity early on, and on her advice I have always kept piano playing as a sad and private pleasure. Many people have had this kind of experience, I think, especially where music is concerned. We become steeped in the notion that if we can't excel, there's little point in pursuit.

I hadn't worked any of this out in an analytical way until my left chest episode caused me to wonder how much longer my sentence would run on. It occurred to me that I had, to that point, been mostly inclined to believe whatever I was told. Perhaps this had been a mistake. Certainly, it had proved constraining. Consider the bassoon. I had wanted to play it for the longest time but had not allowed it as a possibility because I was persuaded I could never be adequate to the task.

But look death in the face, or even see him out of the corner of your eye, peeping around a corner, and you quickly learn that much of what you've taken as gospel can be better summed up with a curt expletive: "Bullshit!"

And why the bassoon? It looks like a piece of plumbing gone wrong. It is cumbersome to carry about. It is temperamental and requires constant cosseting. And it makes a sad sound, like a goose who intuits she is soon to be changed into pillows and drumsticks. All the things that are so outwardly ridiculous about the bassoon are the very reasons I find it so seductive. I don't know how to explain my attraction except to say that the instrument fits me, somehow. It sits well in my hands.

I have never been much of an autodidact. I prefer to have some mentor show me how to do something rather than figure it out for myself. But as there are no double-reed Svengalis near to hand, I have had to teach myself the ins and outs of bassoonery. This I have done with the assistance of a couple of "how-to" books, both of them replete with tunes such as "Flow Gently Sweet Afton" and "English Country Garden" and "The Skye Boat Song." I flatter myself to think that my rendition of "La Cucaracha" could pass muster at any fiesta.

We have a pantry off the kitchen, and it is there that I like to hide away and hone my craft. It is a resonant room, and I can simply close the door and wail away to my heart's content. I annoy no one except Waffle, who likes to sleep on the pantry window ledge and who for reasons known only to herself can't abide my music making. Mrs. Rochester compensates for the cat's antipathy. For reasons that are equally mysterious, she simply adores the sound of the bassoon, or at least the sound I make with it. She perches at the top of the shelves and listens intently, her head cocked, hopping from one foot to the other the whole time I practise. Indeed, it was Mrs. Rochester who was responsible for bringing media attention to my bassoon playing.

Our local newspaper, the *Occasional Rumor*, was founded by J. MacDonald Bellweather in 1920. The *Rumor* of old was a charming little country paper. There was no apparent schedule to its publication. Bellweather had made a killing, one way or another, in munitions. He had no need to concern himself with such irritating and stifling considerations as profitability. The *Rumor* appeared as it was required, sometimes once a week, sometimes twice, sometimes after a month-long hiatus. It carried the news of births and passings. It had hints on the best way to fence a garden to prevent deer from pillaging the lettuce. It had recipes for pie crusts and jams, and lists of blue ribbon winners at local fairs. There were cartoons that pilloried politicians and vague, meandering editorials by JMB, as he was known to one and all. He ran the *Rumor* single-handedly until his death at the age of ninety-seven.

No one could have predicted he would tick along so smartly and for such an impressive span; least of all his son and heir, J. MacDonald Bellweather II. You will recall that he was affianced to our mother and turned down the opportunity to be our stepfather. It had always been supposed that he would one day take over the editorial reins. But the old man showed no signs of dropping in his tracks and evinced no interest whatsoever in retiring. In time, J. Mac II grew weary of waiting for his father to confer succession and left the valley to make another life for himself in distant Toronto. By the time JMB went to his reward, the younger Bellweather was himself collecting the pension, and it was generally supposed that the *Rumor* would die along with its founder.

But we were wrong. Soon after the old man shuffled, we learned that his son planned to return to the spawning ground and keep the *Rumor* afloat. We all surmised that he meant this undertaking as a hobby for his retirement; that he would preserve the status quo and continue to issue a paper that was gentle, whimsical, and idiosyncratic. Wrong again. He set about immediately to effect a thorough and alarming transformation. Out went the old printing press, which was a notch or two above a church basement mimeograph. In came "desktop technology," and all its many possibilities. Gone was the *Rumor's* familiar format. In came a tabloid-style paper, and tabloid-style reporting. "SEX SCANDAL ROCKS FARM!" shrieked the headline of a story describing the unsuccessful insemination of some cows with a product coaxed from a bull with a low sperm count. "BARBER'S BRUTAL BLOODBATH!" proclaimed the tall type over a single-paragraph account of how Abel Wackaugh, who operates a combination barber shop and hardware store, had sneezed while shaving a customer and nicked his ear. It is unlikely that such an occurrence would have merited coverage had the wounded party been anyone other than J. MacDonald Bellweather II.

The old and much-lamented *Occasional Rumor* was a one-man operation. The senior Bellweather, who was not inclined to delegate, did all the writing, editing, and typesetting, and saw to the niggling details of classified placements and circulation management, too. But his son, who wanted to devote his energies to setting and maintaining high standards of production, decided to hire Altona Winkler as a part-time reporter.

Altona is very much one of the family. Her deepest connection is with Hector, and he must tell the tale of how their union was forged. I will say only that she is a woman of substantial charm and vivacity who makes her living selling soaps and beauty products up and down the valley. Her real calling, she feels, is as a writer, most particularly of romance novels. She was thrilled to be offered cub reporter status at the *Rumor*, seeing it as a way of garnering both experience and credibility. She felt that blinkered, recalcitrant publishers would be more kindly disposed to her steamy epics if she could demonstrate, by way of a by-line, that she was a tested and approved commodity.

Altona's gothic sensibilities, which dovetail nicely with the younger Bellweather's sensationalist proclivities, have served her well at the paper. She is adept at taking a perfectly ordinary turn of events and pumping them up with the breath of scandal:

SECOND PLACE WINNER CRIES FOUL IN PIE JUDGING!
DID ELVIS CURE HER MIGRAINES?
FLOODED BASEMENT BLAMED ON FAMILY CURSE!

Those are just a few of the recent headlines that have beckoned eager readers into her warm, ample, bosomy prose.

Altona is no fool. She approaches her work with an admirable mix of commitment and detachment. She gets caught up in the trajectory of her writing but can also detach herself sufficiently from it to stand back and appreciate its parochial, provincial absurdities.

Still, it was her work at the *Rumor* that brought me and my bassoon a brief brush with notoriety and caused a temporary rift between us. It happened a few years ago. Altona was sitting in the kitchen with Hector, showing him a new line of facial masks. They were made with mud dragged from the rivers of Papua New Guinea. They had never been tested on animals. Altona's Pekingese, Valentine, was lying at her feet. I was in the pantry, working my way through a Vivaldi sonata. Mrs. Rochester was listening closely, as is her wont.

Valentine, however, proved to be no amateur of the bassoon. He would look in the direction of the pantry and whine and groan. I, behind my closed door, concentrating fiercely on my "Allegro Ma Non Troppo," was oblivious to these canine criticisms. Nor did Hector or Altona, who were intent on complexion maintenance, pay him any mind. When his mild complaints garnered no action or response, he tilted back his head and gave way to full-scale howling. I would never have thought that so tiny a skull could be so full of resonators. It was an unearthly, sirenlike wail. I opened the door *tout de suite* to see whatever was making such loud sounds of protest. Mrs. Rochester, irritated by the interruption of her concert, flew from her perch onto the little dog's back and landed him a sharp nip.

She didn't draw blood, although she easily might have. Parrots are powerful of beak. But she was stern enough in her remonstration that he howled even louder than before. Altona grabbed Valentine and rushed from the house in a flurry of hair, feathers, and cosmetic aids.

A hastily cobbled together issue of the *Occasional Rumor*

appeared the following morning. "PERNICIOUS PARROT PIQUES PEKE!" it announced. The story was illustrated by a blurry, closeup photograph of what was identified as the wounded nape of Valentine's neck but might just as well have been a portrait of a centipede. An editorial called for a valley-wide inquiry into the keeping of dangerous pets. There was a recipe for chicken *cordon bleu*, in which the word "chicken" had been replaced with "parrot, or other jungle bird." It was altogether unfortunate.

It took the better part of a week for all the various feathers that had been ruffled to be smoothed. But soon enough, Altona was back with more skin toners. Praise God, we are by and large a reasonable folk. Our passions may be quick to kindle, but our memories are short. This is not a place where grudges come to harbour. And now, I will go to the parlour and bang away at a few scales. I am so pleased I found the bassoon. It does my heart a world of good. ✿

Gordon

For a long time, I never saw the humour in the phrase "I found myself lost." As in, "Halfway down the road of life, I found myself lost in a dark wood." The irony only hit home when it happened to me.

I remember when. It was about a month after the morning I looked at myself in the bathroom mirror—I was shaving—and saw I had turned into my father. It gave me a start. But on reflection (no pun intended), I saw it was inevitable. I'd patterned my whole life on his. Even as a little boy, I knew I'd follow the trail he'd blazed. Study hard. Go to law school. Work like a sonofabitch. And that's what happened.

Through his old boy connections, I got articles with a big downtown firm. I became an associate, worked thirteen-hour days, seven days a week, was a partner by the time I was thirty. Somehow, I managed to meet and marry a woman who didn't mind that her husband was a stranger. She was content to raise our two children without any assistance or input from me. Other than that required by biology. It was a way of life. We chose it. In our own way, we were happy.

One partner in the firm was an attorney whose only passion, other than law, was the great outdoors. She loved nothing more than heading into the wilderness with a kayak, a compass, a Swiss army knife, and a bar of bitter chocolate. She was fierce and used to getting her own way. It was at her suggestion—or insistence—that the senior partners in the firm came to the rather extraordinary agreement that we would go off together one weekend for a wilderness adventure.

"The organization that directs these retreats is used to dealing with inexperienced outdoorsmen. They won't throw you into impossible situations. You'll be challenged without being in danger. And there are group activities that will help us learn to work together in new ways. It'll be a growth experience," she said, cracking her knuckles. An impressive array of sinewy cables ran the length of her forearms.

So we came to this island: seven lawyers with six-figure incomes. None of us had ever seen any of the others dressed in anything but business attire. We arrived at a lodge on Friday evening and were advised to retire early. The next day would be hard slogging.

On Saturday morning, we were wakened before dawn, fed a spartan breakfast, herded into a large 4 x 4 van, and driven along a rut-ridden logging trail. Halfway to nowhere, and halfway down the road of life, we disembarked and stood under the dwarfing trees, listening to the instructions of our wilderness leader, a lean young man called Solstice.

"Welcome to the forest! Tomorrow, you'll be spending the whole day alone here! Today, we'll be doing some preparatory exercises! First, we'll seek out the inner wilderness. Go into the bush, as far as you feel comfortable! Crawl along the ground. Feel the earth with your belly, like a snake! Taste the soil, like a worm! Hug the trees, like a bear! Howl, like a wolf! Ask Nature to tell you her secrets. Come back in twenty minutes, and we'll share our experiences."

None of us looked at the others. Only the partner whose brain-child this was demonstrated immediate enthusiasm. She flung herself on all fours, threw back her head, ululated to the rising sun, and scuttled into the undergrowth. The rest of us wandered, rather disconsolately, into the tangle of green.

I walked for about five minutes: directionless, overwhelmed by the sense of being an alien in this place. The natural world was utterly foreign to me. I couldn't name any of the plants or trees I saw around me, except to say: Conifer. Moss. Fern. The silence was unsettling. When had I last been alone with my thoughts? There was nothing to listen to but birdsong and the useless hum and rattle of my own brain. In the distance, I heard a strangely accented yapping. One of my colleagues, I supposed, getting into the spirit of the exercise.

I was in the woods. But I felt completely at sea. How, I wondered, had a group of hard-nosed professionals been so easily sold this New Age bill of goods? Why were we risking life and limb to please some neo-pagan park ranger wannabe? "Arf, arf," I muttered under my breath. I threw my arms around the wide girth of an indifferent-looking tree. Why not? There was nothing else to do.

"Okay, tree," I said. "Give! Tell me something I need to know." I snickered. But I didn't let go. It felt good, much to my surprise, to hug this tree, which was old and full of the stuff of support. It was unexpectedly settling, like being anchored and buoyed at the same time.

A few minutes passed, and still I held on. The tree was a pine, or a fir, or a cedar. For me, the distinctions are hazy. The bark was raspy, slightly sticky. Resin. I breathed in the smell of Christmas.

"Tell me," I said, again, "tell me something I need to know."

This time the tree spoke. Its voice came up from its roots, rising up through its tight and many rings. It said, "Get the hell out."

If you've heard a tree talk, you'll know that you don't argue or cross-examine. You do what you're told.

I was not in prime condition. It had been a long time since I had run. So, I was surprised it came so easily. Fleet footed and full of wind, I raced over the thick carpet of needles, jumping roots and dodging branches, pelting back towards the trail. I had forgotten that in my athletic high school days, when I had competed in track events, I would drive myself on by grunting out a syllabic rendition of the Lone Ranger segment of "The William Tell Overture." Memory lives in our muscles, though, as much as in our skulls. As I pushed forward, I found myself singing, for the first time in twenty years, "Nunga nung, Nunga nung, Nunga Nung Nung Nung!"

I was elated, strong, invulnerable. I leapt out of the woods, running on velvet paws, a rekindled fire in my belly and groin sparking me on. The van was empty. There was still no sign of my colleagues, who were out in the trees looking for what I had somehow found. Solstice was nowhere to be seen. I didn't pause to consider where I was going or why. It was unimportant. A tree had given me instructions, and I was following them.

I followed the ruts left by logging trucks, running faster and faster on the downhill grade: foot and ankle, shin and knee, thigh and pelvis working on a single circuit, my arms pumping like the surprised Icarus, chest heaving. It was as if I had a whole herd of bison in me, stampeding with a collective death wish towards the edge of a cliff.

I reached the point where the logging trail intersected with the main road—morning mist rising up from black asphalt—considered for a second the option of left or right, and collapsed like a diseased lung.

And that was where Hector found me, curled up foetally on the grassy narrow, my face scratched by branches, my left ankle swelling. It had twisted beneath me when I fell.

"Thought the worst," he said, once I had come to. "You wouldn't win any beauty contests just at the minute. What happened?"

And I told him the whole story, sparing no detail. Had someone suggested to me, only a day before, that I would both hear a tree talk and confess the hallucination to a total stranger: well, I would have said he was mad. Nonetheless, there I was, clutching a thermos cup of black coffee in my shaking hands, blood drying on my face, a pulsing pain running up my leg, telling this Good Samaritan that I had been hearing voices in the forest.

"It said to me, 'Get the hell out.' I guess I hadn't thought about where I was getting the hell out to."

Hector let this settle in.

"Maybe," he said, "you misread the punch line."

"I'm sorry?"

"In my experience, which is slight, trees say just what they mean. No more. No less. It didn't say 'Get the hell out of my forest.' It told you to 'Get the hell out.' That's something else again. Get it?"

I was too exhausted, too sore, to take much of this in. I shook my head and took another gulp of coffee.

"No," I said, "I don't get it at all."

"Not to worry. It can take a long time. Speaking of time, your friends must be out of their minds with worry. Up that road?"

I don't have much recollection of what followed. I was too drained to feel anything like shame, or even interest, in what might happen next. My colleagues were, as Hector predicted, quite frantic by the time we rolled up to the van. No doubt they had enjoyed all kinds of bloody imaginings: Bears. Cougars.

I had become entirely passive. I sat in the cab of Hector's pickup while he negotiated my immediate future. The other partners looked from me to him and back again. We never spoke. I gave them a halfhearted wave and a wan smile. I don't know what he told them. In the end, though, I was brought here, to the Bachelor Brothers' Bed and Breakfast, and installed in a comfortable bed with an ice pack on my ankle.

"My brother, Virgil," Hector said by way of introduction. "Virgil, what book would you suggest for someone who was told by a tree to get the hell out?"

Virgil considered this for a long minute or two.

"Not Dante. But the Hardy Boys might be a good bet. And give him a whisky, quick. Whisky's curative properties are diluted by half if it's given after noon."

That was the first of my several visits with the Bachelor Brothers, two years ago now. I stayed on for four days, reading about the adventures of Frank and Joe in secret passages and hidden caves, in smugglers' coves and lost canyons. In my waking hours and in my dreams, I shared their perfect lives, their well-ordered and moral universe where nothing changed and trees were never known to talk.

On the Monday afternoon, I decided I would change my name

and move to Mexico. But the next day was Tuesday. Ever noticed how the world can seem different on Tuesday? I decided to go back to my family, back to the firm, and begin the hard and real work of getting the hell out. Hector drove me to the ferry. When I stepped from the truck, I caught a glimpse of myself in the side mirror. The cuts on my face were largely healed. I hardly recognized the man who looked back at me.

That's what happened to me. No one will believe any of it. Sometimes, life's like that. ♠

On Love and Skincare

We accommodate up to ten guests at a time. Although there are sometimes large groups who descend (such as the recently departed Raymond Chandler reading circle), the majority of our visitors arrive solo, or two by two. Like to the ark.

Typically, people stay between five and seven days. They are mostly strangers to each other, and it is interesting to watch them build a community. Who knows what makes one cluster different from another? Chemistry, I guess. What's sure is that they're never the same. Sometimes, they become a contemplative order, exchanging not much more than good morning pleasantries and mild remarks about the weather. Other groups are hot and electric. They banter, they spark, they make as much noise as a bunch of after-the-show chorus girls in a dressing room. On rare occasions, we see the signs of real animosity. Last month, for instance, a high school guidance counsellor (who should have known better) deeply offended a professor of Canadian literature by dismissing Robertson Davies as "a poser and a hoser."

Oh dear! The look on the professor's face! You'd have thought she'd just smelled something rancid. Her glance took in his exposed jugular, and she ran her finger over the serrated edge of her grapefruit spoon. Luckily, she contained herself. But she steered clear of him for the remainder of her time with us. I would never level a direct accusation based only on circumstantial evidence. Still—he is our only guest who has ever reported someone sneaking into his room and squeezing the whole contents of a tube of toothpaste between his sheets.

We almost always learn something from our guests, who arrive with their different ideas and theories. This morning, for instance, a civil servant called Bridget, who is reading Proust (who, by the way, is this year's most-read author at the Bachelor Brothers', don't ask me why), started a breakfast table discussion about early memories.

"I've blotted so much out," she said, "I can hardly remember anything before the age of eight."

"Maybe you just haven't found the right trigger," was the suggestion of a computer programmer named Dennis. "I had a girlfriend who used a lavender bath oil. My grandmother must have favoured a similar scent, because with one whiff I was right back in her house. I remembered all kinds of things—the position of the furniture, the colour of the kitchen, the knickknacks she kept around."

I realized then that I am still very much in touch with my childhood memories. Perhaps this is because we have never lived in a house other than this, and every object is heady with familiarity. I suppose I can attach some specific recollection or story to almost any trinket in the place. There are quite a number of these, now that I think of it. Every so often, Virgil suggests we undertake a wholesale deaccessioning of artifacts. Now and then, I'll agree to a very selective weeding. But overall, I resist. This is one of the ways in which my brother and I differ. He is neat. I am partial to clutter.

I was always a scavenger. Nothing made me happier, as a little boy, than to root through other people's trash. You never knew when you might find some discarded treasure that just needed to be cleaned of the bits of eggshell and coffee grounds to be made good as new. Mother was quite tolerant of this instinct, although even she would arch an eyebrow and sigh when I dragged some particularly foul-smelling foundling home with me. Crippled chairs. Lamps suffering from burnout. Knives that had lost their competitive edge. Mother always said that my lust for salvaging odds and sods everyone else had given up on meant I was destined for a career as either an antique dealer or a social worker. Considering the age of half our clientele and the emotional fragility of the others, I think she wasn't far from wrong.

A bed and breakfast is heaven on earth for someone with my recuperative instincts. Things get left behind. Watches, neckties, valuable first editions: these are returned without delay. But people quite deliberately discard toiletries, such as shampoos, conditioners, and little nubbins of soap, just because there is an insufficient quantity left to make it worthwhile lugging home. I know many delicate souls who would not deign to avail themselves of a hair product that had lived most of its life in the shower with a naked stranger. But I'm not shy about turning such items to my own use. Little makes me happier than trying a new shampoo. Over the years, I have laundered my locks with the juices of the aloe vera and the yucca plant, with potions made from honey, apple cider vinegar, whale placenta, and the hard-to-find ooze of some species of sea urchin, collected at great peril by divers off the Great Barrier Reef. I am quite used to being complimented on my hair. Lustrous, soft, manageable, thick, full of highlights: these are the terms of endearment I hear all the time.

Of course, these compliments often come my way through guests who are amazed that Virgil and I, as twins, are so utterly unlike one another when it comes to hairline. Virgil has very little left on top. He grows his fringe long on one side and combs it over the bald pate. He holds these thin strands in place with a staining oil. I have told him that I think this is a big mistake.

"You don't think you're fooling anyone, do you? Why don't you just accept that you're bald?"

"I'm not trying to fool anyone. It's a style, nothing more. In any case, Hector, you are hardly in a position to point accusing fingers when it comes to discussions of vanity!"

He can be touchy. But in this case, he is also right. I *am* a vain person.

It was largely through my vanity that Altona Winkler worked

her way into my heart. She came here about twenty years ago. At that time, land prices in the valley—which have latterly sky-rocketed—were depressed. Altona, on the other hand, was basking in the afterglow of a really terrific divorce settlement. She was able to buy herself a little hobby farm and was freed from the necessity of ever working again. But as she is not the kind to simply cool her heels, she began to write romance novels and to sell cosmetics door to door. Thus far, she remains unpublished. But her career as a beauty product saleswoman has been an unparallelled success.

We met when she appeared on the porch one morning, her case of samples in hand. She asked for "the lady of the house."

"I regret to report that there is no lady. Unless, of course, you count the cat and the parrot. And 'lady' would be stretching it a bit for either of them. You're selling something?"

"Soaps, powders, facial masks, bath oils and salts, skin toners and conditioners, mild astringents, and so on. Perhaps you'd be interested in choosing something for a lady friend."

"Hmmmm," I said, noncommittally. "I've always envied women their cosmetics. There are so many of them! Men have to get by with just soap and a rough towel."

"Not necessarily," said Altona, sensing she had a toe in this unlikely door. "Show me the law that says a man can't use a skin cream! Show me where it says that wrinkles are manly! If you're interested, I'll show you some really wonderful creams right now!"

And that was the beginning of my association with Altona Winkler. It has gone on for a long time now. It suits us both. It is relaxed and casual. Comfortable. In one way or another, we attend to each other's needs. There have been times when her work with the *Rumor* has caused a bit of tension. But we get over it, soon enough. We will never run out of conversation. There will always be another moisturizer to try.

Altona likes to read to me in bed, from a novel in progress. Sometimes, it all sounds alarmingly familiar. Here is an excerpt from *Passion's Sweet Tempest*, which even now is making the rounds of publishers:

> They lay side by side, exhausted by the rigours of love. Anna-
> lise rose from crumpled sheets that were as white and scal-

loped as a meringue. She turned on her elbow and stretched, languorous and sensuous as a leopard. The air around her was heavy with dusk and musk, and still electric with love. She peered across the bed at Umberto. Even without her glasses she could see the thick mat of hair that spread between the rosy mounds of his nipples, like interference on a television screen stretching between vertical and horizontal hold. She watched his chest move up and down, like a bellows: a bellows that had only recently fanned a raging fire. A *frisson* of desire ran through her as she surveyed his Sicilian profile: a profile that bore a striking resemblance to the achingly familiar outline of his country of origin.

Annalise reached out and caressed him. She traced the line of his nose. His pores—they were just ever so slightly enlarged. She knew she could do something about that. "Umberto," she whispered, her tongue near his ear. "Annalise," he exhaled, and turned to her. The whole night lay before them. There was much they had to do . . .

I wish Altona well in her writing career. But I confess it has occurred to me that if one of her novels ever sees the light of print, I might have a hard time living it down. Isn't that life, though? It's full of consequences, and chickens coming home to roost. Here endeth the lesson. ♠

Carl

I keep a family photograph on the dresser at home: four generations of menfolk smiling out of a plexiglass frame. It was taken last year at Christmas, at Eric's place. Eric's my son. The tree is in the background, tinsel, lights, and coloured balls. We stand behind my father, who is in a wheelchair. I hold my grandson, Christopher, eight months, in the crook of my right arm, my left hand on Father's left shoulder. Eric is beside me, both hands resting on his grandpa's right shoulder. We look like wingless guardian angels. Everyone's smiling, even the baby. His grin is toothless and lopsided. So is his great-grandfather's. That's what a stroke does for you. It can change your disposition, too. It made my dad mean. I'm glad he managed a smile—maybe it's a grimace—for the picture. He died New Year's Day, and we all agreed it was a blessing. It was time.

Still, it throws you for a loop, losing your last parent. Even if you're sixty-something, it makes you an orphan. You're a bit more alone in the world. There's one less person for you to please. And, of course, it brings you face to face with your own mortality. It doesn't matter how much you've thought about it. It's unsettling. When I look at that picture, I know very well who, in the natural scheme of things, will be the next to go. Is it a mere coincidence that I signed up for an older men's exercise class at the Y? Or that I've started taking two aspirins a day, even though I never get headaches? I don't think so.

Sorry! This sounds grim. What I really want to say is that I've been thinking, especially since coming here, that it's not so rare for life to work itself out like literature. Everything's so random while it's happening. You think it's all rough edges. But when you look back on the big picture, you see there's symmetry. The tag ends get tied up.

What I've just told you is a good example of that. Christopher is born. A new life begins, just as another ends. And that my father should die on the cold, bleak first day of a new year—well, if you were making it up, isn't that how you'd write it? Simple and moral and complete. Like a children's story, really.

It was Kimberly, my daughter-in-law, who suggested that reading to Christopher would be a good grandfatherly thing. He must have been about six weeks old at the time. I thought this was hurrying it a bit.

"It's not as though he'll understand anything," I said.

"Maybe not. But he'll see the pictures. He'll hear the words. He'll get the idea that books are fun. It's a good idea to start reading to a child as soon as his eyes can focus."

Kimberly belongs to the generation that has turned "parent" into a verb. I shrugged and said I would. What could it hurt?

As it turns out, I like it. I don't know if it does any "good." I mean, I haven't seen any indication yet that little Christopher will grow up and find a cure for cancer just because we've been reading to him. But I don't suppose that's really the point. I enjoy it mostly because it gives me something to say to him. Babies make me feel awkward that way. You can only coo and goo for so long. It becomes pretty one-sided after a while. A book, even a simple one with one word to a page, gives you something in common.

I never made the time to read to Eric. I wonder if he thinks about that when he sees me with my arms wrapped around his son. I wonder if he's surprised to learn his old man is such a ham. I had no idea myself. I never knew I made such a good "MOOO!" Or that I could bark like a dog so convincingly that I frighten the cat. It helps that I actually like the books. So does Christopher, especially the cardboard ones. He's teething.

Now that we're comfortable with each other and have each other figured out a little better, I read him stories that are older than he is. It's more interesting for me. Usually, he puts up with it. I bought him a set of Beatrix Potter. For some reason, he's especially fond of *Mr. Jeremy Fisher*. Me, I like *Peter Rabbit*. When we got to *Peter Rabbit*, I realized that although I knew the basics of the story—who doesn't?—I'd never actually read it before. I also realized that I'd never had camomile tea. I went out and bought some. It turns out I hate camomile tea. Now I know.

Maybe I have this thing about rabbits because my favourite book is *Goodnight Moon*. I think Christopher likes it, too. You must know it. There's an old lady rabbit who's putting a little rabbit to bed. They go around the room and say goodnight to everything they see. The brush. The bowl of mush. The old lady whispering hush. It's a simple, simple story, and very gentle.

We read it for the first time not long after my father died. I am not a sentimental person, not in any way. But I'm damned if the line about that old lady whispering hush didn't open up the floodgates. Christopher just sat there, getting wet from the top for a change. He let me get it out of my system. He's a patient little chap. I like him. ♠

A Vigil

Running a bed and breakfast is an intensely practical and compartmentalized affair. Into each day's short span must be slotted a great many domestic tasks: cooking, cleaning, mending, marketing. The satisfying and consuming rigours of housekeepery rarely allow us time for reflection or inward looking. So, of necessity, these little accounts of our goings-on are set down late at night, when the dust of the day has settled; or first thing in the morning, before it has been stirred up.

Hector's constitution is such that he prefers the graveyard shift. I am more inclined to write in that neither here nor there time of between 5 and 6 A.M., when my mind is in a kind of *tabula rasa* state. It has ever been thus, although I have no idea why it should be so. I suppose it has something to do with circadian rhythms, those regulatory pulses that make our various clockwork mechanisms so individual and particular. In this present instance, however, I am flying in the face of what nature intended. It is late, late, late. Our guests (there are six at the moment) have long since hit the sack. I am, like the lone horseman in Walter de la Mare's "The Listeners," the "last one left awake."

I don't need to look far to find the reason for my aberrant sleeplessness. I nipped out shortly after eight and went down to our local café, the Well of Loneliness. Our friends June and Rae are the proprietors, and they invited us by for the unveiling of their new espresso machine. Hector was unable to attend, as he had a Morris dancing rehearsal. I made up for his absence by knocking back not one but two cappuccinos. Or should that be cappuccini? Whatever the grammar, they were tasty but potent. And I will surely pay for my stupid overindulgence when I have to drag myself through the rapidly approaching day. You'd think that I would know better.

Still, now that I have simply accepted that chemically induced insomnia will be a fact of the next few hours and have decided that I might as well make the best of it, I find that I am rather enjoying the break from routine. There is a real sense of privilege about being unvisited by sleep; especially when everyone around you is watching dream after dream parade across the backs of their closed eyelids. I feel oddly like a watchman, although precisely what I'm charged with guarding I couldn't easily say.

I went down to the kitchen half an hour ago to get a glass of cranapple juice, which I am told is particularly beneficial for the bladder. I didn't turn on a hallway light. There was no need, as I know the route so well by now, after a lifetime of climbing up these stairs and down again. I noted, as I have often done since childhood, how the night turns familiar objects into shape shifters. The rounded crown of the newel post at the top of the stairs might have been a gargoyle, the table in the hallway a donkey, the umbrella stand and its tenants something rare and subaquatic. I was put in mind of the words of Coventry Patmore:

How strange at night to wake
And watch while others sleep . . .

Hector teases me about the way I can align a snippet of poetry with any occasion. He has pointed out that every so often, in the middle of a quotidian conversation, I will slip into iambic pentameter. Hector, I am bound to report, has a passion for embellishment that sometimes gets in the way of the absolute truth. But it is true that I have always had a kind of *idiot savant*-like gift for learning verse by heart. It is harder for me now than it once was, given that a certain fossilizing seems to be taking place in my brain. Still, I have set myself the task of learning all the Shakespeare sonnets by the

55

time I am sixty, and I am more than halfway through the sequence now.

I love the phrase "learning by heart," especially when it is applied to poetry, because it seems such a perfect description of the process of memorizing words that have been carefully chosen and weighed and handled. The heart, I think, which is the home of all things rhythmic, is where learned poems go to live. Over time and repeated use, they are folded into one's being, are absorbed by the blood, and feed the rest of the mechanism: more subtle than oxygen, but as vital, in their way. Memorized poems become part of the whole, like reflexes. They surface as they're required. "There is a divinity that shapes our ends," I said the other evening, quoting *Hamlet*, when Altona Winkler was telling us about her new diet plan. She was not amused. But I didn't mean it unkindly. It was an automatic response, like saying "amen" at the end of a prayer.

I was talking about what I perceive as the lost art of poetry memorization tonight with June and Rae, as we toasted their new Cimbali with cup after frothing cup of the brew that has proved so antagonistic to slumber.

Allow me to digress from the thrust of the narrative for just a moment to expatiate on a phenomenon that has rattled the demographic of our little valley over the last dozen years or so. I cannot really say why it has happened, nor do I particularly care; but it is a fact that a great many lesbians have come to make their homes here. They are now among us in sufficient numbers that anyone taking a survey or census would not get a conventionally balanced response.

We are, by and large, a tolerant people. But I would be lying if I said that all the old-timers in the vicinity were blissfully unconcerned when they first twigged to what was going on. It became apparent even to the most blinkered that the many pairs of chainsaw-toting women who were clearing land and building houses were not, in the strict sense of the word, maiden sisters. More than an occasional eyebrow was arched. And from time to time, there were more overt demonstrations of alarm. "CELEBRATED SAPPHISTS BUY ACREAGE" was the oh-so discreet headline in the *Occasional Rumor* when a famous illustrator of children's books and her partner, a well-known harpsichord maker, purchased a property at the north end of the valley.

But all that was years ago. The "live and let live" mentality by which we have so long abided in our little valley prevailed. I am proud to think that, with a few unfortunate exceptions, we proceed through our lives with all due concern and respect for one another; yet with an admirably contained curiosity when it comes to the intricacies of our neighbours' private lives.

From the point of view of commerce, I am bound to say that, were it not for the lesbians, our community would be substantially less interesting than it is. The Well of Loneliness is a case in point. Rae and June are former high school English teachers, originally from Toronto. They met at a weekend seminar called "Follow Your Bliss."

"I think it was the only workshop I ever went to that actually convinced me of something," said Rae about their subsequent decision to take up with one another and to leave their jobs and the city and move west, to the land of the lotus eaters. They came to this island and valley and have been content ever since. It is a happy story. It makes me smile to think of it.

The women subscribe to the "small is beautiful" school of restaurant management. They have seating for only a dozen. They offer no more than two items on their ever-changing menu. And they're open only three nights a week, although they also make their establishment available for occasional evening entertainments: poetry readings, folk music, Red Cross benefits, and the like.

Poetry and its memorization arose when we were talking about the reading given recently by a visiting feminist poet, whose work is complex and brilliant but in no way well served by her oral presentation.

"She never looked up from the page," I complained. "No eye contact with the audience. It was as if she were reading the stuff for the first time. You'd think she'd know her own words by heart."

"I think you're being a little harsh, Virgil," said June over the hiss of the milk steamer. "She was simply insecure. She needed the text as a kind of security blanket as much as anything."

"Anyway," said Rae, "no one memorizes poetry any more. Even when I started teaching school in the sixties, it had gone out of fashion. After all, it's not a particularly useful skill."

That made me bluster.

"Useful? Why does everything have to be useful? Isn't it enough that something is beautiful? I don't think I'm old fashioned or regressive in any way, but I'm glad that I can still call up the poems I learned in school."

"Such as?"

"Oh—dozens! Poe's 'The Raven.' Keats's 'Ode to a Nightingale.' Gray's 'Elegy.' I once won an elocution prize with my rendition of the 'Elegy.' I was ten."

June laughed. "Gray's 'Elegy' at ten? Good grief! I'd have thought you'd have gone for something by Robert Service. You must have been a morbid little boy, my friend!"

"And you think 'The Cremation of Sam Magee' *isn't* morbid?" I countered.

And then the conversation progressed, bumper-car style, to a very heated discussion about death and the survival of the soul. It amazes me that we, as a species, can argue so fervently over something that is, when all is said and done, unknowable and unprovable. Nonetheless, we all arrive at conclusions and cleave to our certainties: that there is nothing but the Void; or that we will find ourselves writing an admissions exam at the Pearly Gates.

Both Rae and June revealed themselves as believers in total extinction. As for me, I have pitched my tent in the camp of those who are sure that something endures. This is not an entirely fanciful belief. It is founded on a kind of half-baked empiricism. I think I have seen the evidence that some part of us lingers, even when the skin and bones have been consigned to the worms or the flames. I owe this certainty to the owners of another lesbian-operated business. Their names are Darlene and Susan, and they run an automobile service station, subtly named the Rubyfruit Jungle.

We have already said that our mother was a gifted mechanic. Neither of her sons inherited or sought to acquire her skills in this regard. We were perfectly content to allow her to minister to our truck, foolishly believing that she would always be here to do so. It was not until after her passing that we were compelled to seek the counsel of the professionals at Rubyfruit. Given our background, we were in no way ashamed or discomfited (as many men our age would be) to turn the maintenance of our ageing pickup over to a couple of overall-wearing automotive engineers called Susan and Darlene.

What *did* surprise me—alarm me, even—was their diagnostic method. They call themselves "psychanics." Rather than lift the hood or hoist the vehicle pneumatically aloft and study its underbelly, Susan and Darlene rely on channelling information from "the other side." Their method is to stand, one on each side of whatever car or truck is in their care, and to place their four hands on the hood above the engine.

"Do you know your truck's name?" they asked, the first time I visited them. This was shortly after Mother's death, and the truck was unaccountably sluggish.

"We've never given it a name. We've never really thought . . ."

"What you think doesn't matter," said Susan, rather sharply. "Your truck *does* have a name."

"And it's Zoe," said Darlene. Her voice was firm and matter of fact. But her eyes had taken on a slightly mesmeric quality and were focussed on some point well beyond the Rita Mae Brown pinup calendar that hung on the wall.

"Zoe?" I asked. "Why Zoe? Why not Bessie, or Lulu, or . . ."

"Shhhhh!" admonished Susan. "Darlene is going to channel Bob."

"Bob?"

"Her late uncle. He taught her everything she knows."

Darlene's brow was dotted with sweat, and her eyes were now rolled back in her head. Her hands trembled, and her voice was thick and hoarse.

"Poor little Zoe," she whispered. "She's missing someone who has passed over. A woman. Very strong. Very connected to the heart of the machine."

"Mother!" I yelped.

"Shhhh!" hushed Susan.

Darlene continued. "Zoe needs to know that all is well and that her friend has not forgotten her. She is in a good place. Zoe also needs an oil change in the worst possible way. And new brake shoes. And it wouldn't hurt to clean the points. Zoe also doesn't like it when her drivers let M and M boxes accumulate on the floor of her cab. That's all. Bob's going now. Bob's going now. God bless you."

And with that, Darlene lurched back to normalcy. She had no

awareness of what had just transpired. Susan quickly jotted down the instructions. A few hours later, the work was done, and the truck—that is, Zoe—was chugging along, ticketyboo.

"Why should it surprise you that machines have feelings?" asked Darlene when I quizzed her about her gift for mechanical mediumship. "After all, we made them in our image."

Nonetheless, I was amazed. And heartened, too. I had always sensed, intuitively, that the soul marched on when the body had fallen. This was an article of faith with me. Still, it gave me a good deal of satisfaction to have my intuition bolstered with so telling a demonstration. Hector merely shrugged when I reported all this to him.

"Perhaps they could ask Bob to ask Mother what she did with the potato masher. I can't find it anywhere."

I cannot remember the last time I stayed up all night. But now, it verges on being over. It is almost 5 A.M. I have just stuck my head out the window to suck back a few lungfuls of fresh, cool air. It will be a clear day. The eastern sky is lightening. I am sure to be a wreck by the time breakfast is done. Perhaps I will be able to cadge an hour for a midmorning power nap. Now, I think I may as well bathe and dress and do something about breakfast. Oatmeal muffins appeal.

But before I get to that, I have a funereal duty to perform, thanks to the good offices of Waffle. She has just deposited a robin, dead and warm, by my feet. The poor thing must have been surprised in the act of snatching an early worm. Waffle looks terribly pleased to have dispatched its little soul to wherever it is that robins go.

Part of me wants to upbraid her for this slaughter of innocence. But I recognize she is just being true to her nature as a cat. So, I will dole out only a mild punishment. I will hold her on my lap and recite to her, in a very feeling way, another poem by Thomas Gray: not as well known as the "Elegy," but apt for the occasion. It's the "Ode on the Death of a Favourite Cat, Drowned in a Tub of Gold Fishes." That should wipe the grin off her puss. So to speak.

"Who will bury cockrobin?" asks the nursery rhyme I learned as a child. In this case, the question is purely rhetorical. ⌂

Virgil's List of Books for
When You're Feeling Low

H. C. Andersen, *Tales*

Andersen's stories are great works of world literature but all too often are regarded as the exclusive property of children. The joy in reading these stories comes from seeing a fully formed imagination in full flight. They remind us of what it is possible for us to do and become. Hence, they are more than stories. They are affirmations.

M. F. K. Fisher, *An Alphabet for Gourmets*

W. H. Auden, who was no slouch, thought M. F. K. Fisher was among the finest prose stylists writing in English. She is celebrated as a food writer, although she said her subject was more properly hunger: the human hunger for love. Mrs. Fisher's abecedarius for foodies is full of sterling, sensual examples of her gift for moving tangentially from the starting point of nourishment into broader and universal concerns. I especially like the chapter "L is for literature" in which she both laments and celebrates the oppressive and invigorating compulsion to read through the ever-mounting pile of available books.

Allan Gurganus, *White People*

Mr. Gurganus is an American writer, the author of a whacking great novel called *Oldest Living Confederate Widow Tells All*. *White People* is a collection of short stories, cast somewhat in the Southern Gothic mode, and I find them very uplifting. For one thing, they are both humorous and wise, which is a rare enough combination. "Nativity, Caucasian" is one of the few stories that has made me laugh out loud. He writes about familial relationships between men—sons, fathers, brothers, grandfathers—in a way that acknowledges the complexities of these bonds but never strays into pop psychology.

Russell Hoban, *The Mouse and His Child*

Who could fail to love a book that features a troop of thespian crows called "The Caws of Art?" This is one of those children's books, like *The Wind in the Willows*, that deserves a wide adult audience. It's the affecting tale of a clockwork mouse and his child who embark on a quest to become self-winding. It speaks very feelingly of the need we all share for home and for love.

Katinka Loesser, *A Thousand Pardons*

This is a small and very beautiful collection of stories by a writer of great skill. The word "prolific" could never be applied to Katinka Loesser. She has published only three books, of which *A Thousand Pardons* (1982) is the most recent. Her stories are too rare, quiet, finely etched, and bittersweet to ever attract a huge following. She will always be a cult figure, an exclusive club, which gives me a kind of selfish comfort.

James Merrill, *From the First Nine*

James Merrill is the greatest American poet of the twentieth century: a technician and a medium of enormous gifts. This representative sample of his work, from the earliest writing until 1976, is one of those books that surrenders something new and previously unobserved on each successive reading. I am especially partial to "The Summer People," a long, sad ballad populated by world-weary sophisticates who bear striking resemblances to some of our guests.

Alice Munro, *Lives of Girls and Women*

I chose this title rather arbitrarily. In fact, anything by Alice Munro would deserve a place on this list. She has never, not once, crafted a sentence that is graceless or awkward. She has never used a word out of place. Her inspiration must come in moments of heated abandon, but her craft has everything to do with careful control. Every story is a surprise, and she has a unique genius for unveiling what's remarkable in the seemingly ordinary lives of seemingly ordinary people. These are books to pick up when you question whether continuance is a viable option. A bright-eyed hope sings from her writing.

Vikram Seth, *Golden Gate*

This novel, set in San Francisco and written in verse, makes me smile every time I pick it up. It's funny, it's brilliant, and it's audacious. It pleases me no end that a young Indian man captured the loopy spirit of California so tellingly and appropriated the rarefied form of the sonnet—one of the great literary achievements of a colonizing culture—as his means of transmission. These are delicious ironies, made the more delicious by the easy way he gets away with it.

James Thurber, *The Thurber Carnival*

This anthology of stories, fables, and drawings was published in 1945. It is significant for me on two fronts. It was one of the books sent to us by our father; and it was one of those transitional books that bridge the gap between childhood reading and adult reading. I felt terribly knowing and chuckled appreciatively at the cartoons, although it's certain I didn't get them at all. They are, after all, quite sexually sophisticated. This is a perfect bedside book, and a great reminder that there is much virtue to be found in simplicity. ♞

One More Year

Virgil and I have recently had our birthday. Don't ask. Fifty-something, suffice it to say. We do nothing ourselves to mark the glorious occasion of our tandem arrival all that time ago. But friends will be friends. And year after year, in their misguided but well-meaning way, one of our associates manages to force a celebration on us.

Altona Winkler was the mastermind of this year's fête. I am very fond of Altona, as you may have gathered. She is a woman of many fine qualities. But sometimes she lacks firmness of purpose. She easily falls under the influence of whatever book she happens to be reading or whatever movie she has just seen. After *Gone with the Wind*, she raced home determined to make a frock out of her drapes. Thankfully, she had venetians. Altona is inclined to bend with the prevailing wind, and just at the moment, her sails are billowed with a biography of Richard Wagner. She was most taken by the description of how, as a Christmas gift for his wife, Cosima, he engaged a small string orchestra to play outside her bedroom door. She woke to hear the lovely strains of a piece he had written especially for her and their young son: "The Siegfried Idyll."

I guess that Richard Wagner was able to put the touch on some pretty fine musicians. I suspect that if the only one available to him were Abel Wackaugh, he would have shelved the "Idyll" and ordered up a dozen roses and a box of chocolates. Just before dawn on the morning of our shared birthday, we were wakened by Abel's truly memorable bagpipe rendition of "Tie a Yellow Ribbon." He stood in the entrance hallway at the bottom of the stairs and played for all he was worth. Exactly how much that would be, I don't care to say. In order that nary a note be missed and every nuance be appreciated, he had also brought along a small sound system. Waves of feedback and speaker crackle wafted upwards, supporting the melody on their zephyr wings. I have never heard anything quite like it. Imagine our surprise! Imagine, too, the delight of our guests—all eight of them—at being similarly roused.

Cosima, as I recall the story, reclined in her bed and smiled a smile of pure enchantment: as who would not, given her circumstances? But no one who was under our roof that morning remained prone. In fact, the hallway leading to the stairs looked like the closing scene from *Casablanca*; or something out of the Thurber short story "The Night the Bed Fell." Who knows what imagined Armageddons enlivened the sleep-dulled minds of these mostly elderly visitors as they stampeded from their rooms and made for the nearest exits, their dentures sloshing in cups and their nightclothes flapping? They looked like panicked horses fleeing a stable fire. Praise heaven, no one slipped as they thundered down the stairs. They ran from the house into the dawn's early light, through the invigorating red glare of the popping flash cubes of Altona's Kodak Instamatic. Never one to pass up a photo opportunity, she was immortalizing the moment for the *Rumor*, all the while shouting "Happy birthday, boys! Surprise! Happy birthday!" It was only when Mrs. Rochester commandeered the microphone and issued her usual curt reprimand that the wailing stopped.

"I'll not be spoken to like that by a bloody parrot!" said the properly miffed Abel Wackaugh, who stomped from the house, trailing bits of wire and tubing and plaid. To say nothing of clouds of indignation.

"Somebody should tell him not to wear sneakers with a kilt," said Virgil as we watched him shove his way through the dazed crowd of golden-agers.

They were, I must say, extremely good humoured about the whole thing, once they understood their sleep had not been shattered by the last trumpet and they were not at the epicentre of the final days. In fact, a distinctly celebratory mood set in. Funny how a sense of reprieve brings that on. Like Gertrude Stein's pigeons, they stood upon the grass, alas, barefoot in the dew, but not seeming to mind. They lifted up their early morning voices and crowed a scratchy but nevertheless rousing rendition of "Happy Birthday." (Can someone tell me how this song became so famous an anthem? It must be one of the dullest and most musically inept tunes ever set down. And hard to sing, too. No wonder it brings a tear to every eye.) Altona stood on a kitchen chair and conducted the *ad hoc* choir. When the applause had died, and a great many kisses and handshakes had been exchanged, she announced that she would make French toast all around. Which she did. And very good it was too, sprinkled with icing sugar and smothered in syrup, with strawberry jam available for those whose inclinations bent in that direction.

The birthday cake she brought out by way of a chaser, thick with frosting and festooned with sticky roses, was maybe—as the French will say, post toast—*de trop*. We all bravely tucked in, though. Another chorus of "Happy Birthday" was sung. This was substantially less clamorous than the first. The excitement of the day seemed to catch up with our visitors at that point. Most of them opted to take their coffee (black, I couldn't help but notice) back to their rooms, where they remained until late in the afternoon. Recuperation is a lengthy business, once one reaches a certain age. As I well know.

I am recuperating even now from a particularly strenuous Morris dancing rehearsal. I am reclining in the bath, in water that is as hot as I can stand. It's frothy and perfumed with fragrant frangipani bubbles. Altona's birthday gift to me was a selection of toiletries, including a very enthusiastic foam. (It was an altogether generous package: mud packs, after-shaves, *eau de toilette*, and an intriguing facial scrub made from ground-up peach pits, seaweed, and honey. I'm not sure if I should wash with it or cook with it. Virgil received a 1500-piece jigsaw puzzle which, when assembled, makes a picture of half a dozen bassoons, arranged like a bouquet, in an Etruscan vase. He was very pleased.)

I believe this is the first time I have ever tried writing in the bath. It's every bit as challenging as reading in the bath, which is among my favourite pastimes. Simultaneous reading and bathing is an art that requires a great deal of practice, if you care to do it well. Any dyed-in-the-wool aquatic reader will tell you that you can't have an enjoyable soak unless you have bubbles and that they should be whipped up until they achieve Everest-like proportions. It has taken me many years to learn how much potion I should add and to recognize the critical moment for pouring it, so that the optimum ratio of froth to liquid can be achieved. It's worth the trouble. What sensation can compare with settling into a thoughtfully prepared bubble bath: the feet, the legs, the loins, the trunk, the arms, the neck, each in their turn passing through the cool and insubstantial foam, each thrilling to the shock of the hot water beneath?

Balancing is another challenge to bathtub reading, principally because the hardware was constructed with cleanliness rather than with literacy in mind. We who are devoted to this recreation know that it can be enjoyed only if we have ready and easy access to some rather particular accoutrements and accessories. A glass of sherry. A tin of Poppycock. A box of Kleenex to wipe the steam from spectacles or to dab away a tear. All these should be near to hand, balanced precariously on tub rims that are really too narrow to afford anything like secure storage. In the back of the mind, then, lurks the nagging and unsavoury prospect that at any minute a whole wad of Kleenex will slide into the deep. This has happened to me on more than one occasion.

There are other risks. Falling asleep, for instance, can be very perilous. Although I believe there have been very few cases of drownings as a consequence of dropping off while in the tub, the book will certainly be in jeopardy. And you have to be careful in your selection of reading material, too. If you're combining your bath with a mudpack, you'd be ill-advised to read something comical and sidesplitting. You'd worry all the time that you'd guffaw and crack the clay and that laugh lines would be permanently moulded in rather than smoothed away. I believe that Kingsley Amis and David Lodge have wrecked many facials in their time.

And if you plan to go directly from your bath to a romantic assignation, you should steer clear of "can't put it down" thrillers or mysteries. Stay in the tub too long, and you will go to your beloved all wrinkled and prunelike, which isn't exactly aphrodisiacal. Or you might find they've given up on you and gone home. Only a couple of weeks ago, Altona threw open the bathroom door and said, "Make up your mind! Is it going to be me? Or Ruth Rendell?"

But tonight, there is no Altona. And Virgil is in bed. So I can stay here as long as I care to, holding my notebook and pen just above the foam (which means that I am writing this in a kind of hieroglyphic scrawl that I very much hope will befuddle some future scholar) and adding hot water as it's needed by manipulating the faucet with my foot: another of the virtuoso tricks I've picked up over the years.

Oh, the years! Tonight, I feel my age. My whole body aches. I think it is entirely possible that Nature, in her wisdom, is telling me that it runs counter to her prescription for a fifty-something man to undertake some new and untried physical challenge. Such as Morris dancing. To be sure, it seems benign enough: exactly the sort of ever so slightly goofy activity a man about to enter his dotage might well enjoy. And benefit from, Lord knows! All that hopping about and bell jingling and handkerchief waving look like the very thing to get the old heart rate up and coax the sluggish blood into the extremities. A jigging pulse and a festive glow: those were the only physical side effects I'd anticipated when I agreed to J. MacDonald Bellweather II's request that I cast in my lot, each and every Wednesday evening, with the Valley Morris Men. As it turns out, it's a damn sight more taxing on the physique than I would ever have credited. And, with Bellweather at the helm, it's no hell on the psyche, either.

J. Mac is in his mid-eighties and looks twenty years younger. Of course, he knows that we know the rather sordid story of how our two families were meant to be soldered but were ultimately sundered as a consequence of mother's under-the-truck indiscretions. We have never spoken of that long-ago incident. By silent, mutual consent, history has been revised in such a way that the whole episode has been wiped from the official record. Nonetheless, whenever I see him (and everyone who lives in a place as small and insular as this sees everyone else with great regularity), I can't stop myself from wondering how different things would have been had he been able to overlook her shortcomings and marry our mother, according to plan. What kind of a father would J. MacDonald Bellweather II have been? Would we have grown like him? What would have won out: nature or nurture?

It is hard for me to imagine J. Mac with children. He is short-tempered, intolerant, and disinclined to suffer fools gladly. On the other hand, I have noted that progeny can have a transformative effect on their parents. And certainly, a child would have given J. Mac a chance to indulge his great passion for toys: for not only does he *look* many years his junior, he has a passion for all that's new in the world of gadgetry that more properly belongs to a young buck.

When it comes to the hasty acquisition of conveniences—those miracles of technology that are meant to make our lives easier—J. Mac has no peer. Witness the way he used desktop publishing to transform the *Rumor* from a quaint and charming country paper to a glossy, offensive scandal sheet. And that is just the tip of the iceberg. His house is chock-a-block with small monuments to the inventiveness of the species, all of which he has eagerly acquired. Electric can openers and pencil sharpeners. Toaster ovens, microwaves, convection ovens. Built-in vacuum systems. Security devices. Cassette, 8 track, CD, video and laser disc players. Ever larger and ever brighter television sets. Ever smaller and ever more powerful home computers. Telephone answering machines. Modems. Faxes. It goes on and on. He has just acquired a video-phone. This has been the source of some frustration, since no one else he knows has similarly indulged himself, and consequently he has no one with whom to play. I can't imagine it myself. One of the great advantages of the phone is that you can make faces at your interlocutor and he'll never know. Needless to say, Bellweather also owns any number of cellular phones.

"Hello, Hector," he barked at me some time back, "this is J. Mac. I'm calling you from the golf course."

Why is it, I wondered silently, that people who call from cell phones always have to tell you where they are? Why did I not feel compelled to say, "Hello, Mac, I'm speaking to you from the kitchen"?

"What are your feelings on Morris dancing?" he asked, coming straight to the point, as is his wont.

"Morris dancing?" I answered, brightly.

He had caught me off my guard. This is not like being asked "Do you believe in God?" Morris dancing had never really entered my thoughts. It had simply never occurred to me that I ought to have feelings for it, one way or another. I vaguely remembered that in *Who's Who*, Edith Sitwell had listed her recreations as "Regretting the Bourbons and avoiding Morris dancing," but long experience has proven that this is not the kind of intelligence to which J. Mac will warm.

"Yes," he went on, "you know. Hats and hankies and hobby horses. Bells around the knees. Lots of jumping around. English stuff. A man's thing. You know."

"Hmmmm," I said. I could smell something in the wind and wasn't yet sure that I found it savoury.

"I've been thinking that it might be fun for us to try. Get a few lads together and see what it's all about. Good fellowship. Good exercise. Thought you might like to join us. You, me, Abel Wackaugh. Maybe that Gill Sinclair fellow from up the valley, seems a good sport. Veterinarian, isn't he? You know. What do you say?"

"Oh, Mac, I don't know. It's getting quite busy at the bed and breakfast, and besides I don't have any bells, and . . ."

"Busy? Nonsense! Everyone's busy. Got to take some time out for recreation. All work, no play. That's what they say. You know. And don't you worry about those bells. Don't need 'em. Bells are passé. I've ordered up these musical computer chips from Japan. Just strap 'em to the knees, and they chime away pretty as you please. Great stuff. Great stuff."

"But Mac—I don't know *how* to Morris dance. And I don't suppose Abel and Gill do either. Do you? Who will teach us?"

"No problem. Ordered a video. Great instructional series. Got Szechuan cookery, too. Wednesday night, say at eight. Suit you? Good. See you then."

And so, for the last three weeks, the four of us have been leaping and cavorting about in front of the huge screen that fills the better part of one wall in J. MacDonald Bellweather's "media centre." The Morris dancers on the video are so enlarged that their pores look like craters. Every so often, in mid-prance, I have a kind of out-of-body experience, where I hover above the room and survey this altogether ridiculous scene: three men in late middle age and one frighteningly fit octogenarian skipping about in a very small space, crashing into one another and the furniture, bruising shins and ankles and egos, waving hankies like children seeing grandma off on the train, and all the while, the irritating chirping of the goddamn chips fills the room. That the Japanese—who gave us the tea ceremony and lovely woodblock prints and judo and Mount Fuji— could also invent such diabolic devices as these proves there is no such thing as consistency when it comes to national character. They must have been designed for those Christmas cards that play a jaunty seasonal carol when opened; novelty cards with a very short-lived charm. "Frosty the Snowman" and "Jingle Bells" and "Auld Lang Syne" are among the dozen or so twittering tunes that fill the air as we try to mimic the movements of the men on the screen. The clash of melodies and the awful tinny sound have made me appreciate our musical eggcups all the more.

"That's the way! Good lads! Hoopla!" shouts the indefatigable Mac by way of encouraging us in this lunacy.

And now, here I am. My whole body aches. I give it another month. By then, Mac will have discovered some new enthusiasm, or we will have engineered a discreet mutiny.

70

"Happy birthday, Hector," he said to me tonight, handing me a large package as I limped towards the door.

It proved to be a "home spa." This is some kind of device you can use to turn an ordinary bathtub into a jacuzzi. Appended to the instructions are a great many caveats listed under the heading: "Danger! To avoid electrocution . . ." It looks very much to me like the sort of thing that will sound like a backhoe. So, I think I will consign it to the basement, to the growing pile of useful dross that will go to the church rummage sale in the fall.

All the heat has gone from my bath now. And nothing is left of the bubbles but the scent of frangipani and a rainbow-coloured stain that will soon be transformed into a blue and clinging ring.

Waffle is mewing outside the door. When the water has drained from the tub, she likes to jump in and roll around, enjoying whatever residual warmth remains in the porcelain. Then she will stare down the drain, in her quiet meditative way, like a mystic contemplating the third eye. Whatever she sees down there, she keeps to herself. I rather suspect it's better that way. I'm another year further along the road. The older I get, the more I understand that there are things I just don't want to know. ♦

Hector's List of Favourite Authors for the Bath

Kingsley Amis
He makes me laugh, and he makes me think. These are two good things to do when you're submerged.

Timothy Findley
Especially the short stories, and *Not Wanted on the Voyage*. Flood epics are particularly appropriate to bathtime reading.

Mavis Gallant

A bath should have something of the elegant about it, and I can think of no writing more stylish than that of the Montreal-born, Paris-based Mavis Gallant. As someone who has never lived elsewhere, I enjoy reading the works of a happy expatriate who feels the strong tug of home.

P. D. James

Nothing like a good police procedural for the bath. It engenders all kinds of pleasantly morbid imaginings about the dire things that might befall one while soaking, and how the naked truth would one day be revealed.

Erica Jong

Oh hell, I'll just come out and say it. Because she has a dab hand at writing about sex, and not many have done it as well. What better to read when you're naked, wet, and warm?

Philip Larkin

Especially good for short soaks, these brilliant, aphoristic poems are smart and melancholy and often funny. I can almost forgive him for writing "Books are a load of crap."

A. A. Milne

I have loved *Winnie the Pooh* since I was a little boy. If I need reassurance that the perilous world contains something worthwhile, it is *Winnie the Pooh* I turn to. My nickname for Virgil, when we were small, was Eeyore. *Plus ça change!*

Carol Shields

What a fine writer she is! Her novels and her short stories, most especially the magical stories in *Various Miracles*, never cease to astonish me. I recommend her for the bath, for the couch, for the armchair, and the bus: indeed, anywhere that reading is possible.

Sei Shonagun

The famous *Pillow Book* kept ten centuries ago by this Japanese noblewoman is full of pithy reassurances that all the pettiness and vanities we know so well were familiar in another culture and another age. This can be comforting when you catch yourself fretting over the state of your cuticles in a postnuclear world.

Oscar Wilde

I have a couple of tubside books made up of his trenchant witticisms. You can absorb a few quips while quickly getting ready for a party, then stun everyone with your rapier wit. ♠

What Gets Left Behind

It is coming on high summer. In homes all across the realm, travel plans that have been roosted on and nurtured during the dark, chill months just passed are now on the verge of hatching. Dreams and schemes of escape are taking on palpable form. Road maps. Agendas. Guidebooks. Fat packages from travel agents. The air is heavy with the gathering heat and with the expectation of good times in the offing. Just last night I had a long hard look at our reservation book and couldn't suppress a little shudder. It appears that an entirely disproportionate number of those respite-seeking, soon-to-be-travellers are steering themselves in our direction. This is flattering, to be sure. But it does make me just a tad uneasy to think that we have become so pivotal in the anticipatory world of all these good people who are, in many instances at least, total strangers.

It astonishes me that this has happened. Why do so many people want to come to a place such as this, where there is absolutely nothing to do but take a walk or two and live the life of the mind? Our accommodations are in no way deluxe. Outward diversions are minimal. There is no bungie jumping nearby. There are no rocks to scale. There is no nightlife, other than folk music and poetry evenings at the Well of Loneliness. I suppose that what we have here is the working out of the adage that it takes all kinds to make a world. But how have so many people found us? We have never once advertised our B & B or gone out of our way to make ourselves known to the world at large. The lesson, I suppose, is that even in this electronic, digitalized, fibre-opticked world of instant communication, there is still a place for Dame Rumour to do her busy work. And that, in a way, I find a heartening thought.

Predictably, summer is our most lunatic season. There is absolutely no chance that we can take part in the time-honoured warm weather pastime of pulling up stakes and going elsewhere. Quite frankly, I am just as glad. I have had occasion to wander in the past, and it doesn't suit me. As I recall, the anticipation of travel was far more pleasant than the actual event: crowded airports, inadequate roadways, mislaid hotel bookings, bottlenecks in museums, uncertain grub, water that is a domicile to all kinds of invisible, hostile bacteria: none of this sets my heart aflutter. Deracination in any form just doesn't suit me. I like my creature comforts. I like the simple dependability of the familiar. I am like a dull ruminant, content to graze in well-known fields and re-examine the same old cud.

One of the privileges of being a helmsman on a ship such as the one we sail is that the world brings its stories to us, and we never have to leave the harbour. In this respect, our innkeeping lives are Chaucerian. We can simply stay put and listen to the tale-telling pilgrims as they pass through en route to a Canterbury of their own choosing.

I woke up this morning and lay curled between the sheets, my thoughts drifting from Chaucer to Mother and back again. These two formidable figures do not usually occupy adjacent bunks in the dormitory of my mind. I attribute their pairing to the two-fold cause of my waking. First, there was the impressive choir of birds that assemble in the trees outside my window each and every dawn to raise their voices and strum their ukuleles and generally indulge in a full-scale carry on. Their morning hymn touched some neuron that opened the door to Chaucer's "Book of the Duchess":

My thought was thus: that it was May
And in the dawning there I lay
(This was my dream) in my bed all naked
And looked about for I was waked
By little birds a goodly number
That had shaken me from my slumber
With noise and sweetness of their song.

And Mother—who is never far from the surface of my thoughts in any case—bobbed up beside Chaucer because just as the birds were urging me to slough off sleep, one of our guests passed by my room, whistling.

Mother was a whistler, both accomplished and habitual. Not for her a tuneless, aimless wheezing: no, she whistled melodic renditions of tunes that might be popular or obscure. She was a virtuoso who could introduce a tremulous warble into the mix or let loose with a trumpetlike blast. We tend to associate whistling with a state of aggravated cheerfulness, but Mother whistled regardless of her mood. In fact, her choice of tune was a reliable barometer of her emotional state. If she puckered up and let fly with "I'm Just Wild About Harry," we knew that all was well with the world. Selections from *Carmina Burana* preceded a fit of domestic frenzy. And for reasons that I was never able to entirely discern, a few of the more energetic *Goldberg Variations* were seismic warnings of an impending eruption. Neither Hector nor I inherited her gift for whistling: perhaps it is controlled by the same gene that administers the passage of mechanical skills. Mrs. Rochester, however, will sometimes surprise us by cutting loose with a very convincing whistled rendition of "Shuffle Off to Buffalo" or the mad scene from *Lucia*.

It occurs to me that it is a fairly rare thing for a woman to be a whistler. Why should that be? Perhaps I should put that question to our musical guest, Joyce. She's an occupational therapist with an avocational passion for birdwatching, which makes her skill at whistling seem both apt and a telling illustration of the ongoing dialogue between art and nature.

Many of our late spring and summertime guests are indefatigable birders. They are a hearty breed of folk who are given to early rising, heading out into the fresh-breathed day with their binoculars about their necks, rucksacks bulging with granola bars and field guides and the notebooks in which they keep their lists: catalogues of birds observed as well as other eye-catching fauna, thought-provoking flora, and meteorological musings.

As Joyce passed my room this morning on her way to the lavatory, her jaunty marching tune was "June Is Busting Out All Over." The birds outside my window raised their voices in general accord. "Summertime," Joyce whistled on her return visit, "and the living is easy!" Hearing that, I could only groan and bury my head in my pillow. For "easy" is not the adjective you would apply to describe the summertime living at an establishment such as ours.

Birders aren't the only keepers of lists. In summer particularly, lists rule my life: lists of everything that requires doing as we gear up for our most frenetic time.

There are small repairs without number that must be made.

There are provisions that must be purchased.

There are linens to be examined, and towels to be monogrammed with the quadruple B, which is the brand we use at this particular ranch.

And then, since we play host to numbers of families, and since it is not unknown for children to be among them, we feel a certain obligation to provide the possibility of some physical recreation. So there are the many toys of summer that must be disinterred from their off-season resting places, assembled, and installed for the amusement of all.

There is the badminton set, whose annual exhuming sets in motion a whole chain of inevitabilities. The net is strung between two conveniently placed dogwoods. Predictably, some shortsighted soul, addled by the sun and possibly by just one daiquiri too many, will try in a fit of vain braggadocio to vault over it at the end of a match and finish up in a twisted sprawl in the middle of the lawn.

Always, several dozen clip-winged shuttlecocks will come to roost in the high foliage therearound and won't be discovered till the trees give up their secrets in the fall. We know, too, that players will be frustrated in their search for rackets. Children will have taken them away to use as banjos and will be off somewhere, strumming them and singing "Oh Susanna!"

Then, there is the deluxe wading pool, a plastic monstrosity with a rod assemblage "so simple even a child can." But there is never a child around when we try to make the thing paddle-worthy. It takes hours to put together. It takes hours to fill. It takes days and days for the sun to warm the water. We know that the first child over the threshold will have a casual relationship with bladder control and that within days the water will be mottled by sunscreen residue, drowned bugs, grass clippings, and the aftereffects of who knows what indiscretions. After a week, it looks so unappealing that it will be ignored by all and will simply sit on the lawn till the season ends; when it is removed, it will leave a large brown ring on the grass, like a crop circle, by way of a souvenir.

We have to repaint the gazebo.

There are Japanese lanterns to be hung along the walkways.

We have to dislodge spiders from the sprinklers and see that our garden hoses have made it through the winter unscathed.

We must take our dull old push lawn mower to Abel Wackaugh, who will sharpen and hone it and ensure that it once again has gay young blades.

And then, when the greens are clipped, we will have to set up the croquet course. We have a stretch of lawn at the side of the house that is the perfect dimension for this sport.

For me, croquet is nothing less than a transformative experience. Nothing sings so eloquently of summer as those mallets, balls, stakes, and hoops. There is no sound so sweet as the cracking report that issues when you thwack your opponent's ball clear into the distant shrubbery. There is no thrill like that of leaving the others in the dust as you move from hoop to hoop with the grace of a gazelle and the accuracy of a surgeon. It is the only game that stirs in me some jungle instinct, that makes me want to beat my chest and gird my loins with the skin of an endangered species and drink blood fresh from the vein. It is the only game that wakens in me something like fury when I lose. Which I almost never do. People who have known me for years but have never seen me in the rabid throes of a croquet-induced passion cannot believe their eyes. I can hardly wait for it to begin. But first, the list of "must dos" has to be whittled down to something roughly approximating the length of my arm.

As oppressive as a list may be when one is a slave to its demands, there is a certain beauty to it; to seeing all the tasks that must be laid to rest all arranged and laid out like a poem. When I get a secondhand book, I like to subject it to a little archaeological dig, searching out the bits and pieces that have been left behind as bookmarks. Often, there are unwanted business cards, or grocery receipts. But it's not uncommon to find lists. Just last week, inside a copy of Edith Sitwell's *English Eccentrics*, I found what I took to be a shopping list consisting of only two items:

Ice
Matches

The conjunction of these two simple commodities suggested so much! I imagined how the list maker had been giving a party and had to make a last-minute run to the store for these overlooked items, so drinks could be chilled and candles ignited. What else might she have forgotten? Flowers? Decaf? Antipasto?

I was reminded, too, of the poem in which Robert Frost wonders whether the world will end in fire or in ice. That set me off on a long deliberation of the advantages of one over the other. I concluded that I would prefer fire, although I very much doubt the question will come up for referendum.

It pleases me so much to find odds and sods that have been left behind in books. This is evidence that books—even bad books—are organic: not just static and moribund repositories for calcifying ruminations. They grow and change as they pass from hand to hand. Here is a sign that readers, as well as writers, share the human need to leave some sign or symbol that we have passed this way. Nothing is more telling of this urge than marginalia: that cramped and often lunatic scribbling that some contentious soul has squeezed up against the sanctioned text.

Marginalialists (if that is what they are called) love nothing better than to correct the grammar of the published. What wouldn't I give to thumb through the library of the fellow whom Virginia Woolf slyly and wryly credits in her introduction to *Orlando*: "Finally, I would like to thank, had I not lost his name and address, a gentleman in America who has generously and gratuitously corrected the punctuation, the botany, the entomology, the geography, and the chronology of previous works of mine and will, I hope, not spare his services on the present occasion."

Here is a partial list of other items I have found left behind in books:

A seating plan for a formal dinner

A twenty-franc note (Belgian)

A coaster from the Algonquin Hotel in New York City—and this was in a biography of Dorothy Parker

A flyer that says "Lose weight now, ask me how"

A matchbook cover, emblazoned with wedding bells and the words "Debbie and Craig, September 12, 1972."

A label, soaked from a ketchup bottle

A receipt from Harrod's, for the purchase of lute strings

And on one memorable occasion, a sardine.

The discovery of these and other foundlings that slip from between pages raises myriad questions. If I were the novel-writing type, I would find any of these evocative traces a sufficient springboard for the creation of some fiction. But nothing has piqued my curiosity so much as this single page from what I take to be a much longer letter. I discovered it in an old treatise on double reed–making that I acquired through a mail order book service in Maine. I have no way of gauging the date of the letter, but I would guess it to be about a hundred years old. The handwriting has a nineteenth-century cast to it. It is neat and precise. But here and there are blots that suggest it was written with some sense of febrile urgency. The page begins and ends in mid-sentence. I reproduce it in its entirety for you.

. . . and it does make one wonder if perhaps Aunt Adelaide was right in warning us we would rue the day we hired a French governess. Of course, we have only the word of little Milicent to go on; and she did see the whole episode through the keyhole. But all the physical evidence—the bottle of Madeira, the Portuguese-English dictionary, the discarded clothing, the mandolin, the heap of ash, the grease spot on the counterpane—seems to corroborate the story. And she is too young and tender by far to have invented so macabre a tale as this. Whoever in their wildest dreams would have expected that Mademoiselle, in spite of being French, could have done such a thing? And who would have so black a soul as to wish on her such a terrible fate, in spite of all her wickedness? I have not been able to sleep these past three nights for thinking of it!

Milicent has just turned eight, and her account is somewhat confused. Understandably, given the circumstances. What seems certain is that Mademoiselle invited a sailor to her room. She must have smuggled him up the servants' stairs late at night. We suppose he was with one of the ships from the Azores, the fishing fleet that has latterly been in port. They must have polished off the bottle of Madeira: from our own cellar, says Winston, who keeps track of such things. Little Milicent, who heard giggling and went to make her keyhole investigation, said that Mademoiselle was "fighting with a man on her bed, and they were both bare naked!"

When they had tired of wrestling, the sailor lay back on the pillow and began to play the mandolin. That set Mademoiselle to capering. She jumped up and down on the bed. She jumped and jumped, higher and higher, and then—and this is where the story strains against every standard of credibility—in the midst of one spectacular leap, when she seemed suspended between bed and ceiling, she simply burst into flames.

I see these words and wonder that so few syllables can convey all the horror of what happened. How else can I say it, except with those few bald words? She burst into flames, and in a matter of . . .

And that is where the letter ends: "in a matter of . . ." I imagine that it went on to say "seconds, she was consumed by fire." But then what? What of the sailor? Was he also engulfed? Or did he leap through the window and scuttle back to his ship and tell his incredulous companions of his adventures?

What are we to make of this? A ruse? Possibly. Or might this be an account, true and authentic, of that most puzzling phenomenon, spontaneous human combustion? Such occurrences, though rare, have been documented in the past.

Perhaps it doesn't much matter. One imagined ending is as good and as valid as another when the facts that might settle the case are unknown. I have had many grim and pleasant hours concocting various aftermaths to this unhappy culminating event in the life of an unfortunate French governess.

But this is not the time for idle imaginings. By day's end, I want to look at my ponderous list of things to do and have the satisfaction of seeing check marks beside half a dozen of them, at the very least. I will begin with polishing the banister. Then, I will test its shiny worthiness by sliding down its length. It's a rash act for a man of my years, and I suppose I'm inviting disaster. Perhaps I'll fall victim to pyrotechnics between the top and the bottom. On the other hand, it's June. The birds are singing full throttle. The season for busting out is on us. ⬆

Sophy

Can we have a word please, *entre nous*, about this parrot? Mrs. Rochester. The rude one. Where does she get off saying the things she says? Did I hear correctly? Was that the "F" word I heard her pronounce this morning when I dropped my toast? I think it was. Whatever happened to "Who's a pretty boy"? What's wrong with "Polly wants a cracker"? Who does she think she is?

Frankly, I have a problem with birds as pets, even when they're well mannered. Something about them gives me the shivers: the beady eyes, the reptilian feet, the unsettling way they turn their heads. No wonder we have the superstition about birds in houses. What better creature to be a messenger of evil?

I came by my aversion early on, and honestly. Our next-door neighbour, one Mr. Bridgman, was a bird-raising enthusiast. He had pigeons in a coop in the back yard. They were inoffensive and cooed prettily. He had canaries and parakeets in inside aviaries. They were attractive and contained. But he also had this parrot, a strangely crested cockatoo called Jacko. Jacko never spoke. He shrieked and howled, like a jungle bird, which is what he was. But this was Edmonton, and his banshee clamour was completely out of place. During the winter, Jacko carried on inside, his owner his only audience. In the summer, though, he lived largely outdoors. This was the base from which he would scream happily into the air and from which he carried out any number of terrorist raids against children who were paddling in back yard wading pools. This activity, for reasons that were known only to Jacko, inspired in him a passionate loathing.

Jacko's wings were clipped. But he was happy to hop from one yard to the next, to sneak through the grass, and surprise us by leaping into a pool, delivering sharp nips wherever he could land his beak. Everyone would scream and run, leaving Jacko to splash around a bit in solitary splendour. Before he moved on, he would leave his calling card: a large, loose dropping, floating in the middle of the water.

We complained to our parents. They complained to Mr. Bridgman. He would cluck sympathetically and promise to upbraid his errant parrot. But the next day, the same thing would happen again.

Jacko had what proved to be a lethal fondness for inhaling the vapour from the oilpans of cars. After he had dispersed the neighbourhood children, he would shelter himself under a Dodge or Rambler and cool down in the shade. I suppose he must have been in mid-nap the afternoon my father got into our Chrysler, backed it down the driveway, and squashed poor Jacko flat.

Mr. Bridgman, unfortunately, saw it happen. He held Jacko in very high esteem, and seeing the life crushed out of his beloved, obnoxious companion was more than he could bear. He was always a slightly marginal character, insofar as mental stability was concerned, and this sad event precipitated a quick decline. The very next day, he removed all the pigeons from their coop. The poor dull things sat puzzled on the fence and watched, along with the rest of us, as Mr. Bridgman dismantled their house, board by board. Then he brought out the several large cages in which he kept his parakeets and canaries. There must have been fifty of the birds, at least. He unlatched the doors, and one by one they understood that they were free. One by one, they took to the air.

When the last of the birds had flown, Mr. Bridgman began to flap his arms up and down, awkward and hopeless. Then he set himself to spinning. Around and around and around, a dervish, he spun and spun, never getting dizzy and falling to the ground, like we did when we played the same game. He let loose a volley of sounds, awful, piercing shrieks. Jacko had failed to acquire human speech, but Mr. Bridgman was a deft imitator of his parrot.

We children were hustled inside. Somebody called an ambulance. For days afterward, we would see unfamiliar flashes of colour in the flat-leaved trees. Eventually, Mr. Bridgman returned to his house. He was very much diminished.

So, I never have liked domesticated birds. Not since that day. And Mrs. Rochester has done nothing to make me feel a welling of fondness. Otherwise, you can count me among your satisfied customers. And I do appreciate the irony that the book I brought along for this little reading retreat was that modern classic by Julian Barnes, *Flaubert's Parrot*. ♠

The Songs of Solomon Solomon

"Rain, rain go away, rain, rain go away." This is one of Mrs. Rochester's regular refrains these days. She mutters it as she hangs upside-down from the curtain rod, peering out through the rivulets that stream down the kitchen windowpane. She chants it, mournfully, while spitting the husks of her sunflower seeds onto the floor around her perch. She punctuates her commentary on the sad state of our summer so far with colossal sighs. And every now and then, when she simply can't stand it any longer and the soggy injustice of it all is just too much for her tropical, sun-loving heart to bear, she lets fly with a really heartfelt "Fuck off!"

Mrs. Rochester is old, and Mrs. Rochester is crotchety. Still, she remains a fairly discreet bird. She rarely brings shame on the family name by belching out this foul oath when visitors are within earshot. I'm always interested to see how guests respond to her occasional slip-ups. Some are alarmed, some are amused. There are those whose faces take on that "let's pretend it never happened" look, as if someone had just broken wind. For all her coarseness, though, Mrs. Rochester is also capable of very elevated discourse. Mother, who had a lifelong fondness for things French, used to delight in teaching her beloved parrot little Gallic aphorisms. Only this evening, Mrs. Rochester set down the celery stick she was reducing to gummy strings and, with a faraway look in her beady little eyes, said, very plainly, *"Il pleut sur la ville comme il pleure dans mon coeur."* It was an apt remark on several fronts, for not only was the weather pluvial; it was the fourteenth of July. Bastille Day.

"Allons, enfants de la patrie!" said Virgil and I together. We were standing in the kitchen, folding bed sheets and doing our best to answer the questions of one of our visitors, a professor of folklore from an eastern university. It was work that brought him here as much as pleasure; although, like many academics, he inhabits an obsessive world where that twain often meet. The project that has brought him to our valley is a study of the works of the poet Solomon Solomon.

You will have never heard tell of Solomon Solomon, but he is well known hereabound: or at least he was, in his time. His writing was published in the *Occasional Rumor* from the founding of the paper until his death in 1959. Solomon Solomon never knew the curse of writer's block. He turned out thousands of poems over the course of his long career. They appeared in virtually every edition of the *Rumor*, sometimes one poem, sometimes several.

It would never have occurred to any of us to attach the adjective "remarkable" either to him or to his *oeuvre*. He was a commonplace figure in a small place. And while familiarity did not breed contempt, we looked on him with that bland, unthinking acceptance that is meted out to prophets in their own country. For us, Solomon Solomon and his prolific output were part of the ordinary landscape. We anticipated the newspaper appearances of his poetic musings with the same certainty we accorded the earth's spinning and the sun's rising. A measure of our genial disregard is that no one ever thought to collect the poems or to publish a selection in a volume. Nor will such a thing be possible, given that Solomon Solomon himself saw his work as ephemeral and left no papers behind. The elder J. MacDonald Bellweather, founder of the *Rumor*, was similarly unencumbered by an archival instinct and never preserved a complete run of his paper.

Consequently, in the absence of a fixed reference point and because the few remnants of his rhymes are widely scattered, Solomon Solomon's reputation has dimmed somewhat over time. Our young people now know very little about him. So we were more than slightly surprised to find that someone from beyond the hills had stumbled upon old issues of the *Rumor* in an archive and deemed Solomon Solomon worthy of wider attention. You can well imagine his disappointment at coming here and finding that a poet whose work he admired was so evidently undervalued by those who should properly hold him dear.

The bed sheets Virgil and I folded were still warm from the dryer and crackled with electricity, even though I had used any number of products that promised they would free the universe from the irritating problem of static cling.

"I don't mind wet weather," I said, as we joined corner to corner, "except that it means we can't hang clothes on the line. There's nothing like the smell of a clean sheet that's been dried by the sun and the wind."

"Where I live," said the professor, "we actually have a bylaw prohibiting clotheslines. Some civic busybodies decided they were unsightly or unsafe or some such thing."

Virgil and I clucked disbelievingly, shaking our heads at this evidence of how governments, at one level or another, just can't resist the impulse to control every aspect of private life.

Virgil said, "It's a good thing Solomon Solomon didn't live in your neighbourhood. Otherwise, he would never have written "The Hedge."

"The Hedge?" The professor opened his notebook and retrieved his pen from its habitual resting place behind his right ear.

"It's one of his poems I have by heart." He recited:

> I stand behind your privet hedge
> And watch your drying sheets,
> And try to think of where you laid
> Your head, your hands, your feet.
>
> I see them billow in the wind,
> These starchy, linen ghosts,
> Pinned upon the line that links
> Those matched but separate posts.
>
> I think of how your sheets, this line,
> Resemble life on earth:
> The line is insubstantial,
> And the sheets, for all they're worth,
>
> Cling upon its thinness,
> Like the spirit to the flesh,
> Punished by the howling wind
> The whole time that they mesh.
>
> They dry for but a little span,
> And when their time is done,
> They're snatched away and taken
> From their season in the sun.
>
> And life, my love, is much the same:
> I shall not be discreet.
> Call me from your privet hedge,
> And let me share your sheets.

"That's quite remarkable," said the professor, after a few

moments of respectful silence. "You can see how he was influenced by the seventeenth-century metaphysical poets. As well as by Emily Dickinson. But tell me—how is it you remember that poem? It must be well over thirty years since you saw it in print."

Virgil looked away and blushed modestly, while I explained his gift of near photographic recall for verse.

"How many poems from the Solomon Solomon canon do you know, then?" asked the professor, looking very much like a man who has just stumbled on the motherlode.

"Oh, I don't know. A few dozen or so. But they're very easy to recall. The rhymes are pretty straightforward, and he wasn't one for experimenting with meter. It's not so very different from remembering a nursery rhyme. And most of the Solomon Solomon poems I know have a family connection."

The professor grew brighter and brighter.

"Family connection?"

Virgil and I looked at one another. We'd neither of us spoken of this, or even thought of it, for a long time. After we finished folding a rather tricky fitted sheet, Virgil explained.

"We think of it as a connection, although we have no direct proof. But it's been our suspicion that Solomon Solomon was deeply, hopelessly in love with our mother, and that his unrequited passion was one of the fuels that fired his work."

"Fascinating! You mean she was sort of a Dark Lady of the sonnets?"

"I guess you could say that," I said, "although I don't recall ever reading a Solomon Solomon sonnet. Do you remember if he wrote any, Virgil?"

"One or two, perhaps, when a maverick mood was on him. But they weren't among his strongest work."

The professor was taking rapid notes.

"And how did you come to believe your mother was his Muse?"

"Oh," said Virgil, "there were a number of clues. For one thing, there was a period of time when he was a very regular visitor to the house. We were quite young, hardly more than toddlers. But it stands out in my mind. We didn't have many people dropping by. Mother never troubled to marry, you see, and the fact that she was a single woman raising illegitimate twins made her more than a bit of a pariah. Solomon Solomon, who had the artist's healthy disregard for convention and respectability, came to see her regularly for a couple of years. Then, one day, he simply stopped calling. Mother never spoke of why. We have always imagined it was because he made a direct proposal and received a direct answer that was not what he hoped to hear.

"In any case, for years afterward, whenever he saw her or us on the street, he would look down, or look away, or cross to the opposite sidewalk to avoid us. And he wore a terribly pained look on his face."

I picked up the story. "Even as kids we could tell he was heartbroken. And it was just at about that time that he began to publish poems that were full of longing and sadness."

"Ah," said the professor.

I peeked over his shoulder and saw him make a note: "starcrossed lovers / internal textual evidence."

"There were times his poems were so close to events in her own life," said Virgil, "that it was impossible not to think that he was writing with her in mind."

"Can you give me an instance?" asked the professor.

"Oh sure. The most transparent example would be 'Madonna of the Valley.' " He declaimed:

> Fair Lady, you are not ashamed,
> Though some may call you whore.
> Those who sling such arrows
> Are the crassest of the boors.
>
> Some have called you miscreant,
> And some have called you communist.
> Just because you suckle both
> A Remus and a Romulus.
>
> But pay no heed, Fair Lady,
> To such calumnies and jibes.
> Know full well there's one who'd like
> To have you for his bride.

Oh come and be my shepherdess,
And all life's pleasures prove!
Live with me, Fair Lady!
Be my dearest, truest love!

"Hmmmmm," said the professor. "Perhaps just a little deriva-
tive. And I'm not sure about rhyming 'communist' with 'Romulus.'"

"There are times when he could have benefited from some good
editing," Virgil conceded.

"Still, the sentiment seems genuine enough. How did your
mother react to these poems when she saw them in print?"

"Oh, Mother wasn't the kind to give anything away," I said. "She
wasn't what you'd call demonstrative. But they must have meant
something to her. When she died, we found the poems clipped and
filed with some other papers in an envelope marked 'DESTROY.'"

"Ah!" exclaimed, his nostrils twitching at the whiff of a new
scent. "And did you . . . comply with her wishes?"

"Of course," said Virgil. "You never knew Mother. She wasn't
the sort of woman you disobeyed, not even in death. The papers
were burned, as per her instructions. But I did take the liberty of
reading through the poems, first. I really can't stop myself from
memorizing verse, so I suppose they found a perch on which to
roost."

"Were all the poems of a similar length?"

"Mostly," said Virgil, after a pause. I could tell he was rifling
through the filing cabinet of his brain, searching for the rule proving
exceptions. "The only poem of any length appeared in the *Rumor*
shortly after Mrs. Rochester's great escape of 1947."

Mrs. Rochester, hearing her name, danced a stiff hornpipe and
muttered, *"Lasciate ogni speranza voi che entrate! Mi chiamano, Mimi!"*

"And this is one of the poems you have in your head?"

"I believe so," said Virgil. "It's been some time since I've tried to
say it, but it must be in there somewhere."

"Would you mind?"

"I'll do my best. You should have the footnotes first, though. You
need to know that Mrs. Rochester was Mother's constant companion. She followed her around like a little dog, flapping from room to

room, or scuttling along the floor. She rode on Mother's shoulder when she did yard work, or kept watch from a nearby tree. Mother never clipped her wings. She thought that to do so would be cruel and unnecessary. Mrs. Rochester came to us unbidden. As far as Mother was concerned, the parrot was a free agent who was welcome to stay as long as she cared to remain. Should she decide to go out into the world again, to seek her fortune elsewhere, that would be fine, too.

"Or so Mother always said. She had a certain investment in appearing nonchalant and cavalier about personal attachments. However, on the day that Mrs. Rochester did decide—for indiscernible reasons that doubtless made sense to a parrot—to go on an extended flight, Mother was as close to tears and panic as we ever saw her. She chased her over hill and dale, and finally snagged her in the village. Those are the facts on which Solomon Solomon based his epic."

Virgil cleared his throat, assumed a heroic stance, and began:

> Oh, it was on a day in June,
> The sun was bright, and dark the moon,
> The air was blue, bereft of clouds,
> And on the rounded earth, a crowd
> Of valley folk looked up to spy
> A flash of green across the sky.
> The valley folk looked up and saw,
> A flash of green, with beak and claw.
>
> "Oh what is this and what is here?"
> They asked. Some turned away in fear,
> While others gaped in frank delight
> To see this unexpected sight.
> They pointed skyward, loudly called,
> "Oh gilded bird, from fairy halls,
> Whence came you here? Oh tell us, tell!"
> The bird responded, "Go to hell!"
>
> "Oh naughty bird!" the crowd exclaimed,
> "How did you come hereby? Explain!

Abuse us not with filthy lines!"
"Stick it where the sun don't shine!"
The parrot shrieked. Oh! How the throng
Winced to hear this crude, lewd song.
How they blushed when next she dared
To bellow out a lusty *"Merde!"*

"How foul the fowl!" the crowd bemoaned.
"Will anyone admit he owns
Such a bird, whose sole directive
Is to spout such foul invective?
And to spout it, what is worse—
Every calumny and curse—
At a sweet and gentle people
From their church's holy steeple!"

Then at that very moment came
A beautiful, though frazzled dame:
Loveliest in all the land,
With a birdcage in her hand.
She was flushed from making haste,
Slender was her willow waist,
Rosy cheeks and eyes that charmed:
Venus, but with both her arms.

"Help!" she begged, "I cannot bear it!
I have lost my precious parrot!
Have you seen her here nearby?"
The crowd rose up and shouted, "Fie!
"Fie!" they shouted. "Fie again!
Fie on you and all your kin!
Fie on those whose birds besmirch
And desanctify the church!"

"Woe is me!" the damsel said,
"I would that I were sick or dead!
Oh! Is there none to call upon
To save my darling Amazon?"

Then there came a clarion call.
Every heart leaped up, enthralled!
"Stand you back and stand aside!
I shall help!" one hero cried.

"Ahhhh!" the noisesome crowd exhaled.
Through their midst, both wan and pale,
Strode the poet with his lyre:
Orpheus, suffused with fire
For the Eurydice who
Never guessed or quite construed
That he loved her better than
Ever loved another man.

He struck his harp, and raised his song.
It soared above the rabble throng,
Soared above the thronging rabble,
Stilled their shrill, discordant babble.
And the bird from deepest Hades—
Feathered, squawking, green escapee—
Held her tongue and listened hard
To the pleading of the bard.

Never was there music sweeter!
Never a more pleasing meter
Than the one the poet spun.
Never had a mortal sung
Such a tender, touching ballad.
And the poet, thin and pallid,
Reached the hearts of all that heard:
Even the alarming bird.

With his rhyming he assuaged,
Coaxed her back into the cage,
Coaxed her down, becalmed and quelled,
To the cage the fair maid held.
"Thank you, sir," she said, "you're kind.
Never did I hope to find,

Once my bird had taken flight,
Someone who might reunite

Bird and woman. Thanks, indeed."
Then she turned, and with good speed,
Draped the birdcage with her cloak,
Fled the village and its folk,
Fled the rowdy, mocking horde,
Fled without another word.
"Woe," the poet cried, "is me!
She's a *belle dame sans merci!*"

He never heard her speak her name,
Knew not whence the lady came,
Knew not where she kept her cot,
Where she'd built her sad Shalott.
From henceforward he would pray
That they'd meet again one day,
On some near and distant shore.
Quoth the parrot: "Nevermore."

Directly Virgil finished this long narration, he collapsed into a chair, flushed and breathless. I saw him furtively check his pulse. The professor was duly impressed.

"That's truly remarkable! Something of Poe, something of Long-fellow, and a *soupçon* of Browning, all blended together into something that is distinctly Solomon. I must say I'm astonished that your mother had no interest in pursuing a relationship with a man who cared so deeply about her. To say nothing of one who was so poetically adept."

"Mother," I explained, "had only had one great love. It didn't work out. There were incompatibilities. Family. Geography. The same old story. I think she decided early on that if she couldn't have the man she wanted, she would do with no man at all."

"Ah," said the professor, kindly and sadly. "And that would be your father, then."

Virgil and I simply sighed, enigmatically. It was too convoluted a tale to get into, there and then.

In spite of the complications that surround locating the texts of Solomon Solomon's poems, our academic visitor has decided that he will embark on a full-scale study. He thinks that it might turn into his life's work, and for that I am glad. Discovering one's life's work is a good thing to do, regardless of what stage of life you're at.

Our present guests—all ten of them—are early-to-bedders. The professor was the last to hit the sack. Virgil followed shortly on his heels. I stayed up late, with Mrs. Rochester, to write this. I wanted a nightcap to stimulate the creative juices. In the fridge, I located vermouth and just enough gin to make one martini. There was also a jar in which two lonely, pimento-stuffed olives bobbed up and down in their salty brine. I transferred them to the gin. When they were thoroughly saturated with the essence of juniper, I ate one and gave the other to Mrs. Rochester. She held it delicately in her scaly claw and sucked out its red heart before gobbling the rest.

I wondered if she had ever before, in her long life, tasted gin. It occurred to me, rather belatedly, to wonder if it might be harmful to parrots. But she showed no ill effects. She grew quiet and contented, as though she were looking inward and remembering her glory days of long ago. "Nevermore!" she chuckled once, and then gave herself over to parroty dreams. ♠

Recipe

Muffins without Peer

This recipe was given to us by the writer and broadcaster Margaret Meikle, an occasional visitor to the Bachelor Brothers' Bed and Breakfast. We know of no better way to use bananas that are just ever so slightly over the hill.

Cream together:

    $^1/_2$ cup margarine

    1 $^1/_4$ cups brown sugar

Mix in:

    2 eggs

    $^1/_2$ cup oil

    6 mashed bananas

Add:

    3 cups flour

    1 tsp. baking powder

    $^3/_4$ tsp. nutmeg

    2 tsp. baking soda

    1 tsp. cinnamon

    dash of salt

    optional fruit—dates are good

Bake at 350° Fahrenheit for 25 minutes, or until you're good and satisfied. This makes 12 muffins. ♠

Now We Are Two

Sometimes people ask, "What's it like, being a twin?" This is a tricky question for which I have no adequate answer. After all, I have never been anything else and have no point of comparison. The best I have been able to say is that when you're a twin, the conjugation "we are" sits more easily on the tongue than "I am."

I wish I could find a more satisfactory riposte, something less abstract and foggy-minded. I can remove myself sufficiently from my life and circumstances to understand the curiosity and fascination single units have for we who are the product of a fallopian freakishness. Many people—at least, many of the slightly confused and gentle souls who come through our doors—spend their lives trying to heal a rift, the source of which is a mystery to them. They feel both a profound separateness and a longing for unity, as though they are part of a matched set that was broken up long ago. They have no memory of this sundering; only the firm, instinctual conviction that it happened and that something is missing.

This is the human condition, this hungering after wholeness. It lives in everyone at some level of knowing. There are those who have dragged this deep-seated need from the subconscious to a more active plane of awareness and who think that twins are born lucky; that we come into the world with a ready-made Other, with a known shadow already in place.

I have been taken up with these existential musings thanks largely to our friends Rae and June, the proprietors of the Well of Loneliness. They have devoted many of their weekends to attending New Age workshops of one kind or another. "Fear and Empowerment in the Nuclear Age." "Accessing Angels." "The Tarot and Macrobiotics: The Mayan Connection." Only yesterday, they stopped in for tea and told me about one such session on "Rebirthing." I'm not entirely sure I understand the principle, but I gather that through a series of breathing exercises and marginal-sounding regression techniques, participants are meant to re-experience the trauma of leaving behind the warm, wet world of the womb for the nasty, brutish business of strutting and fretting, getting and spending.

"Why on earth would you want to go through it more than once?" I asked.

"For emotional ownership," said Rae.

"And healing," said June. "You can't imagine what it's like, that first gulp of air. It fills your lungs, top to bottom. And it stings like hell. No wonder we bellow."

"I don't have any trouble with the idea that you experienced something," I said, "but surely you don't think you were remembering your birth!"

"Why not? Why shouldn't we be able to remember it? After all, it's the primal experience. It must make a big impression in the moment."

"Hmmmmm," I said, rather dismissively.

The conversation moved on to other things, and I forgot about rebirthing, which I took to be implausible at best. Nonetheless, I can only suppose that a seed was sown; for last night, I had a vivid and peculiar dream. I saw myself—no, *felt* myself—bobbing like an astronaut in space, floating free but anchored too, connected umbilically to his silver craft. The atmosphere around me was foreign, but in no way hostile. In fact, I felt very much at home. Nor was I alone. I was curled about another being. We were separate but at the same time linked: aspects of one another, shared selves, nestled like spoons, like yin and yang. I had the distinct sense that we two were talking between ourselves, not in words but through a process of thought transfer; though what it was we were saying, I can't imagine.

It was a lovely, peaceful, floating revery. I could have happily stayed there forever. But Waffle jarred me out of it by leaping onto my chest and swatting my chin. I lurched into wakefulness, gulped air, and—this is true—felt a distinct burning in the base of my lungs, as if oxygen were reaching a place it hadn't been in a very long time.

It lasted only a moment. I lay there, adjusting to wakefulness, stroking the meddlesome cat from head to tail while she kneaded my breast. I squinted at the digital clock and saw that it was 4.37. In twenty-three minutes, the alarm would kick in. There was no point in restaking my claim to sleep. I would get an early start on the day. I got up, dressed, and went downstairs into the kitchen, where I said good morning to Mrs. Rochester. She scuttled back and forth on her perch, watching me take the muffin batter (rhubarb strawberry) from the fridge, fill a dozen cups, and consign them to the oven. Mrs. Rochester, who is accustomed to receiving tithes, took the strawberry I offered her with nary a word of thanks or nod of acknowledgement, hulled it daintily, and tucked in.

I went onto the back porch to study the dawning day. This has been the wettest summer on record. It had rained most of the night, and while this was a moment of respite from the ongoing deluge, the sky was quilted with clouds, and the air was heavy with the promise of pouring.

I stood there, surveying our small damp kingdom, smelling the imminent rain and meditating on my dream. I felt almost embarrassed. Everything about it was transparent: its source, its meaning. Still, I couldn't help but wonder if it was rooted somehow in memory. Was that what it felt like, that season before birth? So tranquil? So becalmed? Did Hector and I, as peas in the pod, gossip back and forth, whispering over the constant thudding of our mother's heart, the rumble of her intestines?

I thought, too, and not for the first time, about what an extraordinary woman she was. That she bore twins out of wedlock, kept them and raised them, in defiance of every social convention of the time, astonishes me still. True, it was more possible for her than for most other women of her day. She had the advantage of both a house and an assured income: advantages she passed on to us. Nonetheless, she was largely ostracized and left with a rough row to hoe. It would have been so easy for her to give us up, farm us out, turn us over to an adoption agency, and just get on with her unencumbered life.

How would our lives have been different? Would we have gone to separate families, in different towns? Would we have travelled through our days, haunted by the nagging certainty that we were incomplete: not the same angst that we feel by simple dint of being human, but something even more unsettling because it would be, in a literal way, true?

Every so often I read stories about reunions between twins who were separated at birth. Inevitably, their lives are marked by remarkable coincidences. Both will have been named Tom. Both will be chartered accountants. Both will have married physiotherapists called Jean. Both will prefer the same brand of scotch. Both will play lacrosse. Both will live, in their respective cities, at 301 Pleasant Street. And on and on.

Of course, the question this begs is: How much are we given, and how much do we acquire? Had Hector and I been raised apart and then brought together again, as though in a nineteenth-century novel, how would we know one another, or divine our profound connection? Not by appearance, certainly. Would we discover that we both had cats called Waffle? Rude parrots called Mrs. Rochester? Would we both be bibliomaniacs? Would we both tremble when we hear the word "gazebo"?

Ah, the gazebo! Shabby locus of our shared shame! Sad evidence that while we owe all of the accrued benefits of nurture to our mother, that which can be attributed to nature was passed on through our unknown, peripatetic, and evidently impractical father.

In order to appreciate the gazebo, you need to know that we do not have a television. Indeed, we have never had a television. I do not say this proudly or with any of that snobbism that usually attends such revelations. I have nothing against television, *per se*, although I think its overall effect has been detrimental rather than beneficial. I don't rule out the possibility that we might one day acquire one. But for the nonce, we don't see the need.

Altona Winkler, however, is quite a big fan of the tube. She has a satellite dish behind her house that picks up a bewildering number of signals. When Hector overnights at her place, they often channel graze together.

"Which one of you works the remote?" I asked him recently, when we were having a close and brotherly chat. But he blushed and declined to report on that detail of their intimate life.

One night, when I can only suppose that his senses were dulled by postcoital bliss, they saw a "do-it-yourself" gazebo kit advertised on some kind of mail order shopping channel. As Hector tells the story, it was Altona's idea that he should pick up the phone, without delay or sober consideration, and dial the 1-800 number.

"Wouldn't that be lovely?" she evidently asked. "How pleasant for your guests, to be able to sit in the shade of a gazebo and read, or talk. Or play Scrabble."

Scrabble is Hector's game, his bloodsport. He is ruthless and almost unbeatable; which is a good thing, as his occasional defeats precipitate major league pouts. No doubt the combination of the tender circumstances of the moment, a certain amount of brandy, and the alluring possibility of turning Scrabble into an outdoor event pushed Hector over the edge. About this, I can only speculate. What I know for sure is that several weeks after the call was made— a call about which he neglected to inform me—a large truck pulled into the drive and disgorged the four long and heavy boxes that contained the pre-fab gazebo. Imagine my surprise. Hector, too, seemed somewhat nonplussed.

"Hmm. Hmm," he said, over and over, as he dragged the murky swamp of his mind to retrieve the circumstances of the thing's ordering. Eventually the whole story emerged. There have been times when I have been more pleased.

I looked at the bulky crates and saw so clearly what their future was to be. I saw so clearly how they would sit on the grass for weeks on end; saw so clearly how Hector would catch me in a weak moment and inveigle me to help him attempt its assembly; saw so clearly how the "easy to erect" structure would fight us at every turn, how we would sweat blood trying to interpret the instructions, how we would wind up with a bucket full of seemingly necessary parts that we had not managed to situate in the gazebo, how it would crumble under its own weight the moment a slight breeze passed through its portals.

There are times when I curse my own prescience. For all came to pass as I predicted. Within a day of its creation, the gazebo lay on the ground like a Greek ruin. In desperation, we fell back on the habit of a lifetime and did what came naturally: looked for a capable woman to get us out of trouble.

We summoned Darlene and Susan from the Rubyfruit Jungle. They hurried on over, physicianlike, with their little black bag full of tools and a Ouija board. Darlene took one look at the heap of lumber that had had a short life as a gazebo and gave a low whistle.

"Boy! You guys really know how to screw things up!"

"There's a strong spirit presence here," said Susan. "Someone, or something, is trying to come through. We'd better make sure that nothing is going to create interference before we reassemble."

They sat down in the rubble of our making, knee to knee, and held the Ouija between them. No sooner had they settled their fingers on the palette than it began to dart like a hummingbird about the letters. I wrote down the message as it was communicated.

"This is your mother. Where did I go wrong? A simple little thing like a Tab A, Slot B gazebo, and neither of you has the wit to manage it. Lord knows I tried. I did my best. I thought that summer we spent building the tree house would teach you a thing or two about rudimentary construction. Ha! I should have known. You couldn't wait to put down the hammer get back to your fairy tales. I blame your father for that. At least you have the sense to call in competent help. And by the way, I'm sure that neither of these two girls would think to build a gazebo right on top of a sprinkler head. I have to go. I'm having a drink with Leonardo da Vinci. He has an engineering problem I can help him with."

And that was the end of the message.

"Do you really think it was her?" Hector asked, later that night as we sat in the reassembled and relocated gazebo, gin and tonics in hand. It had taken Darlene and Susan a scant forty-five minutes to put things right, once they decided the spiritual air had been cleared.

"Who else? I can't imagine how Darlene or Susan would have known the story of the tree house."

The tree house summer to which Mother referred took place over forty years ago. The tree house itself, still in splendid condition, straddles the spreading limbs of a chestnut tree that shades the far margin of the lawn. I imagine it must have been just this species of tree Longfellow had in mind when he wrote that dreadful poem about the blacksmith. The little hut is about ten feet up. It is reached by scaling a ladder made of small planks that have been securely, if rather cruelly, nailed into the trunk.

When we decided to open our home as a bed and breakfast, the insurance agent we consulted suggested we would be well advised to tear down the tree house. She said that it was "an accident waiting to happen." She made all kinds of Cassandra-like prognostications. Children would climb up and tumble out. Bones would be dashed. The lawsuits would come as thick and fast as locusts. We considered her counsel and chose to ignore it. The construction is still sound. Mother built things to last. And whereas I don't deny there is a possibility that someone might take a fall, I don't subscribe to the theory that children should be overly protected. Needless to say, every reasonable precaution should be taken to keep them from harm in a world that grows more dangerous by the minute. But bumps and bruises and even fractures are a part of growing up. And I have great faith that none of our clientele would point the finger of blame at us, in the event that one of childhood's small and inevitable sadnesses should befall their progeny in our tree house. Call me naive. But that's how I feel.

I also have empiricism on my side. All our young visitors play in the tree house, and none has come to harm. Indeed, I am the only one to have ever fallen from it. And that was not when I was a tad. I regret to report that this happened only last week.

I was out barbering the grass, pushing our old hand mower round about the base of the tree, when I overheard two little ones—the children of a lawyer couple who have become summer regulars—playing in the house above me. It was evident from their voices and the morsels of conversation I could overhear that they were in the midst of a telephone game. Hector and I used to do this very thing. We attached two empty tin cans to a wire and used one as the speaker and one as the receiver. Of course, we could hear each other perfectly well without this phony phone, as we were separated by a distance of no more than four feet. But reality was immaterial. The game, the fantasy, was the point.

I remembered how deeply children become immersed in their play, and though I hated the idea of the spell they had cast being broken by some brutish adult intrusion, nostalgia got the better of me. I couldn't resist the urge to creep quietly up the ladder and stick my head through the opening, just for the selfish pleasure of seeing how childhood is a continuum and how the old ways persevere, even in these dangerous end years of the century.

Imagine my surprise, when I poked my head through, to see that they were not using tin cans and wires but cellular phones; and to understand that they weren't talking to each other but rather to friends back home in Toronto. I felt as though as I were watching my whole childhood quivering on the end of a harpoon. I let loose my grip and fell to the newly cut lawn beneath.

One of the children leaned out and asked, rather kindly, "Should I call 911?"

"I don't think that will be necessary, thank you," I answered.

The wind was knocked out of me, but I was otherwise undamaged. I lay on the ground for about ten minutes, in spite of the accumulated damp, studying the shapes of the clouds as they passed overhead, appreciating the heft of the tree and the rare chance to view its leaves from this underbelly perspective. I turned on my stomach and looked for four-leaf clovers. There were none. I watched a few ants going about their chores. Then I got up, stretched, brushed the clippings from my jeans and sweater, and followed their industrious example.

I have a natural tendency to be self-deprecating, to portray myself as a hapless clown. I am not without my competencies. I do think I play the bassoon rather well, given my late start. I am a very good baker: the muffins this morning were roundly applauded by our guests, one of whom even said she'd rather have such a confection than sunshine. And I am quite good at flower arranging. That is what I will do now, by way of bringing this long day to a close: gather some blossoms to brighten the breakfast table.

That we have so lovely a garden is thanks to the good offices of Altona Winkler. She is an avid horticulturalist. It is work for which she has a real talent: an inborn sympathy for things botanical.

"Novels and gardens," she says. "I like to move from plot to plot."

She favours old-fashioned flowers: lady's mantle, columbine, sweet peas, Canterbury bells, snapdragons, hollyhocks, and, wittily, row on row of bachelor's buttons. She is outside weeding even now, singing at the top of her lungs. She has been reading a biography of Edith Piaf.

"*Non, rien de rien! Non, je ne regrette rien!*" is her repeated refrain.

Singing is *not* Altona's forte. But the garden seems to thrive on it. And even if I have heard that song more deftly interpreted, I am happy to be reminded of its philosophy: regretting nothing and living for the moment, even when the world is drenched and the Lord seems to have forgotten that rainbow promise made so long ago. It has just now struck me how close "rien" is to "rain." Is this significant? Perhaps. But it's a meaning that someone else will have to decipher. I've unravelled as much of the universe as I care to, just for the moment. ✿

Thomas

First of all, a big and heartfelt thank you to the two of you from the two of us. I mean me and Brutus. We've both had a very satisfying visit. For my part, I'm delighted that I'll never again have to confess that I've not read *The Mill on the Floss*. And Brutus—which I acknowledge is a name better suited to a Doberman than a Scottie—was very pleased to have such long, unrestrained rambles. He'll be disappointed to return to Vancouver—land of heavy traffic—and find out he's got the same old leash on life.

Good of you to arrange such accommodating weather, too. It's about time. I don't think I can remember a more heartless summer, even by West Coast standards: cool and reserved, altogether dispassionate. Every week, some unannounced low pressure front trundles in from the Pacific. They come like a parade of newly widowed aunts. All of them have weepy tales to tell. They stay too long and are soon indistinguishable one from the other.

In the city, everyone seems to be in general agreement that there has never been a summer quite this unpleasant. Strangers exchange long and baleful looks in bank lineups or at intersections while waiting for a light to change. We have all been united in a spiritless communion of misery. It is typically a silent bond, although sometimes words of blame are exchanged: volcanoes in the Philippines, the dwindling ozone, the Goods and Services Tax.

Oh sure, there have been rare days here and there when the minor star that keeps us warm and whirling has sung out bold and big and brassy as Merman. But by and large what is meant to be a season of browning has become instead a time of generalized whining. You have to be alert for those small, hope-inspiring reminders that though the prodigal sun remains cloistered behind clouds, he is still doing his work. The other afternoon, when I was taking a break from George Eliot and was out exploring with Brutus, we found a big blackberry patch not so far from here. The hard green nuggets that blackberry flowers leave behind have started to purple and soften and sweeten, as they can only do when the sun has given them a warm massage. In a few days, they will be entering their prime. I expect I will find the same is true back in Vancouver, which means there'll be good eating soon.

One of the joys about having a dog in the city—apart from the ready availability of unconditional love—is that you have to undertake an enforced walking regimen. I owe my discovery of the thriving urban blackberry culture to little Brutus and his insistence that we get out and explore those few remnants of wilderness that remain within the city boundaries. The blackberry bushes are located here and there, along the peripheries of various beaches, along railroad tracks, and in a few parks. We walked past and among the spiky shrubs for some time before I twigged to what they were; and it took me more time still to get up the nerve to actually pluck the oozy, bumpy fruit and ingest it.

I do not come from a family that cultivates, hunts, or otherwise forages for food. We shop. I can identify any number of comestibles when they are lying in state in a produce department or when they are wrapped in plastic or embalmed in labelled jars and tins. I was raised urban and have continued to live that way. The idea of dealing with primary food sources, when it has occurred to me at all, has always made me squeamish. Gardening equals dirt, sweat, and the possibility of wasps or other stinging insects. And the prospect of actually going into the wild and culling edibles from some plant set down by a force as capricious as nature wakens all manner of childhood fears about poison berries. I still cling to the notion, acquired early in life, that the more luscious seeming the berry, the greater its toxicity.

I would probably have never ventured my first taste had it not been that on one particular day last summer—which, by the way, was a *proper* summer, hot and languid—I saw an elderly but exceptionally hardy woman standing in the midst of the hitherto feared

105

and unidentified brambles. She wore a wide-brimmed hat, heavy boots, and thick gardening gloves with the ends cut off to expose just her fingertips. She was plucking the berries with great alacrity and plopping them into a very large bucket. It was her second such container: the first, full to overbrimming, was at the edge of the thicket.

It is a sad commentary on our world that I do not feel comfortable initiating a conversation with a woman who is alone in any place that is even slightly remote from view. To do so typically engenders fear and suspicion, and we need not look far to know why. I would never have spoken to her, had she not shouted out a question about my dog. We fell to talking then, and of course the conversation turned to her particular enterprise.

"What a lot of—er—berries you have there. What do you do with them?"

"Blackberry jam, blackberry jelly, blackberry fool, blackberries and cream, blackberry pie. Just about anything you can do with a blackberry. Tried making wine once, but it didn't turn out. I've been coming here for ten years now, and this is the finest crop I've seen. Here! Just look at the size of this one!"

She held one beneath my nose. I could hardly do otherwise than hoist it into my mouth. It was a revelation. Sun warmed and juicy, with a flavour and texture like nothing I'd ever tasted, sweeter than a strawberry, oozier than a raspberry, leagues away in every respect from a blueberry. The scales fell from my eyes. Life was better than it had been only a few moments before.

From that day forward, my walks with the dog took on a more definite sense of purpose, although I hasten to add I was never as purposeful as my mentor. I never actually went into the long stretch of blackberry bushes with a bucket or even an empty yogurt container. Untroubled by any sort of conserving instinct, I am interested only in instant gratification and eating till satiation. Shallow lad that I am, I nevertheless learned something about blackberries and about the subculture that gathers them. As to the latter, few are as forthcoming as my tutor. Most pickers tend to be rather grim and disinclined to chat. They do not welcome distractions from the task at hand. For the most part, blackberry pickers seem to require a great deal of personal space. If they are working on picking some clump clean, it is generally not a good idea to stray within fifty feet or so of their working area. To do so is unlikely to provoke outright hostility but a certain bristling can be discerned, and if you were to step into a leghold trap or some other contrivance, they would think twice before summoning aid.

It is not so very difficult to understand why blackberries inspire these rather fierce demonstrations of territorial imperative. Each ready fruit is a prize worth fighting for. Furthermore, they seem to ripen in small congregations, while all around them are berries that have not yet seen the light. In fact, although a bush may be sagging with berries, there will quite often be only a few ready candidates for eating. I suspect that some pickers return to the same bit of greenery again and again, day after day, and come to regard it as their own.

For a mere hobbyist such as myself, one of the greatest accomplishments is being able to determine by sight or by a delicate squeeze which blackberry is ready for heaven and which would be best left another day or so. Even a few hours can make the difference between a tang that makes you pucker and a sweet flow of juice that makes you think that this must have been the fruit of the Fall. To stand on tiptoe and reach up through the forbidding armour of a tall blackberry bush, teetering precariously on the edge of balance, and bringing to your mouth the tender morsel that some other picker has either missed or not been sufficiently intrepid to snag, is an achievement not to be sneered at.

Inevitably, there are wounds. In fact, even now my hands are marked with the scratches and jabs from thorns: injuries that will be common once the season sets in for good and for certain. Today, we had a kind of rehearsal for what's to come. For, although most of the blackberries are just beginning to hint at what they will soon become, I found at the very top of the brambles, where the earliest, unshaded berries ripen, one particularly promising-looking cluster. The berries—there were maybe a dozen all told—ranged in shade from deep purple to licorice. I began to sample them. They were palatable but a day or two shy of readiness. Then, I plucked one that proved a tiny package of sweetness, the very definition of ripe. It was heavy with blood and trembled on my tongue like a willing sacrificial victim. The molars came together and did their awful, necessary work. And in that moment, I had one of those rare glimpses when you realize that the body and soul are welded together for a reason.

Brutus was oblivious to my pleasure. He was sniffing for rabbits or mice but failed to find any. I think we'd like to come back next year. But perhaps we'll book a time a week or two later in the summer. I'll have better blackberrying. He might have better hunting. And, of course, I'll look forward to the reading. *War and Peace* or bust. ⌂

The Morning After

The worst injuries are those we bring on ourselves: the booboos that are visited on us through carelessness or unalloyed stupidity. The thumb whacked instead of a nail. The ankle twisted when stairs are taken too quickly. The lap scalded by a carelessly held cup of coffee. And most galling of all, the drumming, brow-splitting, sick-making headache that follows a night of alcoholic excess. The hangover is surely one of the most exquisite and excruciating incarnations of self-inflicted suffering. I woke this morning to the sound of one knocking insistently at my skull, with all the determination of a pileated woodpecker. I had no choice but to let it in. I have been its host this whole day, and a very bad guest it has been, too.

I pray that any devout believers who might read this will tolerate my observation that God, while he may be just and good, is also a trickster of the first water. His creation is full of cruel jokes. Take tobacco, for instance. He provided us not only with this lovely plant but with the inventiveness to see how it might be dried, rolled, burned, and pleasurably inhaled. He did all that, and then went on to make it carcinogenic.

Similarly, consider the grape. Here is a fruit that ripens slowly, achieving a state of self-actualization on the vine, growing into selfhood, beyond reproach, entirely adequate in and of itself. It needs no tampering or outside interference in order to perfect it. In its natural state, the grape is entirely benign and user friendly. For the invention of the grape, in all its many forms and aspects and gradations of hue, now let us praise the Lord!

But let us shake an admonishing finger at Him, too. For He saw fit to burden us with this cumbersome intelligence that causes us to stick an oar in where no oar is needed. We stir things up and make a mess. Not content to let the grape speak for itself, we subject it to all manner of abuse, in order that we might coax it beyond itself. Crushing. Bottling. Corking. Fermenting. Swilling. And for what? A few hours of loosened inhibitions, followed closely on by a night of troubled sleep, and the whole next day lost to a thudding head and a gnawing nausea.

When the pox-ridden sailor was asked how he came to such a sad and sorry state, he answered, "I should have stayed at sea. Port was my poison." I, too, am a victim of port.

I know very well that I have no one to blame but myself for my excesses and their consequences. *Mea culpa*, a thousand times over. But some atavistic, lizardly part of my brain keeps trying to lay the responsibility for the whole beastly business at the feet of the four members of the Jane Austen Society who are presently our guests. These women—friends of very long standing—have a regular booking with us. They come here each September. They make a retreat to enjoy each other's company, to reread *Emma* for the umpteenth time, and to carry on in the way of Janeites the world over.

In addition to their interest in Austen, they share a passion for cookery and can be counted on to take over the kitchen to fix feasts of the food Jane herself might have enjoyed. They are good enough to invite Virgil and me to join them, which we are always happy to do. A joint of beef; potatoes roasted in drippings; Yorkshire pudding; peas and carrots boiled, in the time-honoured English way, into squishy submission; sherry trifle: these are the delicacies, nostalgic and largely discredited from a dietetic point of view, that our guests prepare for their Austen revels. There is a certain guilty pleasure that comes from eating such things: rich, greasy, and heavy. A kind of licentiousness settles in, a sense of invulnerability in the moment.

"Another glass of port?"

"Oh, why not?"

"*Encore du porto?*"

"Maybe just one more."

"How do I like it? Any old port in a storm, I always say! Bottoms up!"

Before you know it, you're taking part in a game of charades and doing all manner of unseemly things to communicate the idea of *Persuasion* or *Sense and Sensibility*. And then the morning comes.

The only good thing to be said about today is that there has been no need to summon up the will to work. Our guests—who could hardly be called "demanding" even when they are at their perkiest—are also feeling muted and have confined themselves to quarters. Every so often, a low moan emanates from one of their rooms. Virgil, who was alone in cleaving to moderation, has been playing soothing, rather melancholy melodies on the bassoon. From time to time, he ferries us all cups of mint tea and occasional wry words of encouragement.

"I've thought up a medical joke that might make you feel better. Want to hear it?" he asked, as he delivered a fresh pot of herbal brew round about lunchtime.

"Gghhhwowownnn," I said, trying vainly to form a full-fledged word, let alone a coherent sentence.

"Okay. Here goes. What did the doctor's rebellious dog say to his master?"

"Unnngghhhhhoowwww," was as much of a response as I could manage.

"Physician, heel thyself."

"Nuuuuhhhhgggwwooo," I said, trying to sound appreciative, but not making much of a job of it. However, Virgil laughs at his own jokes with such enthusiasm that I don't suppose he noticed. Altona dropped by an hour or so ago and wasn't in the slightest way sympathetic.

"Serves you right," was her curt dismissal. "Staying up till all hours, drinking with strange women. A man of your age ought to know better."

And she is right. Altona is always right, just like Mother was always right. This suggests something uncomfortably Freudian to me, which I'd rather not think about at the moment.

Days like this make me powerfully glad that I rarely suffer the ravages of a hangover. Not any more. In my youth, before I had learned the wisdom of moderation, I was much more prone to them. Indeed, I became so expert at their management that over time I learned to chart the course of their progress. I could tell when the headache had reached its peak, its apogee, and would begin to recede, dwindle in intensity. Now, after all these years of running our bed and breakfast, I know that I will experience much the same feeling in the week or so before Labour Day—which has recently come and gone. In those latter days of August, all the accumulated bustle and business of the summer seems to build and build, like sound waves ganging up for a sonic boom. And then, in the twinkling of an eye, something shifts. The fever breaks. A semblance of normalcy settles in. By the dawning of Labour Day, we can breathe again.

For the most part, we both get through our crazy season with a fair degree of equanimity. Occasionally, one of us will start to fray around the edges. But we know the danger signs in ourselves, and in each other. Virgil will start to recite the poetry of Sylvia Plath at inappropriate times, and with a bit too much conviction and vigour. And I will break into a cold sweat at the sight of eggs. Hundreds and hundreds of eggs come under my scrutiny every summer, and they become a kind of symbol of oppression. If I could discover who first decided that eggs are the ideal breakfast food, I would write a strongly worded letter to his descendants.

It's ironic that I should be the one who is principally responsible for the preparation of the eggs each morning. I can only suppose that this is some kind of karma working itself out, some punishment for an unspeakable act committed in an earlier incarnation. For while I appreciate eggs as objects and admire their sturdy construction and spherical splendour, I cannot abide them as a foodstuff. It has ever been thus. It's simple enough to conjugate my aversion. I do not like eggs, I have not liked eggs, I will not like eggs. I do not like them fried, poached, boiled, baked, shirred, coddled, scrambled, or omeletized. I do not like *huevos rancheros*, devilled eggs, eggs Benedict, frittatas, eggs foo yong, or soufflés. I do not like them sunny-side up or over easy, or as an accompaniment to sausages, bacon, or ham. Have I made myself clear? I do not like them, Sam I am. But I have learned to cook them in every possible way and to every possible consistency in order that our guests might leave the breakfast table smiling. Usually, this is compensation enough, and save for those days when I teeter on the edge of the abyss, I bear my yoke gladly. You should pardon the pun.

When the news about eggs and cholesterol first came out, I allowed myself to harbour the foolish hope that the demand for these hen-made treasures would diminish. No such luck. Bed-and-breakfasters want their eggs in the morning, cholesterol be damned! The role played by the egg in the mythology of a place such as ours is pivotal, to say the least. Other than fire, flood, or earthquake, I can imagine no greater calamity than some kind of labour unrest among the poultry, some contractual squabble that might bring about a work stoppage. And that is exactly what happened to us, right in the middle of those few frantic weeks in August.

Every now and then it has occurred to us that we should keep a flock of hens and grow our own eggs. But the logistics of such an enterprise, on top of everything else, are sufficiently daunting that we have chosen instead to subcontract, as it were. For years now, Virgil has made a daily trip to collect brown, white, and spotted eggs from our neighbour, Max Janzen. He has a small farming operation a mile or so down the valley. We like Max and have come to rely on the free range output of his feathered dependents. His business feeds our business, and vice versa. It's been a mutually beneficial relationship. So naturally, we shared his concern when the normally prodigious output of his happy hens began to fall off. Over the course of a few days, it turned into a trickle, until finally a virtual drought fell over the henhouse, and we reluctantly had to go farther afield to supply our needs. We still felt a strong loyalty to Max, however, and called every day to see if his workers had come to their senses.

"Can't figure it out for the life of me," said Max, who was at his wit's end. "The vet says there's nothing wrong with 'em. At least not that he can find. But they don't look quite right to me. They seem kind of—depressed. Know what I mean?"

I didn't really. I haven't spent enough time around poultry to be able to appreciate the subtle nuances of their moods. It only occurs to me that a chicken looks depressed when I see one plucked and hanging in the butcher's window.

"I just can't think of the reason for it. Their grub's the same as it always has been. Only change has been that Jeremy's taken over the feeding."

Jeremy is Max's son. He is seventeen and is home for the summer from the city where he boards at a facility for bright but rather sociopathic young people. In less enlightened days, I think we called them "reform schools." Jeremy is not often seen, but he is frequently heard. He is the proud owner of a very powerful portable sound system, a "ghetto blaster," and it is his constant companion. It's about the size of a dishwasher, and he carries it about on his shoulder. When it is cranked up to full volume, which is where he likes to keep it cranked, it shakes the earth like a herd of bison.

Virgil, who is musical, thought to ask Max if Jeremy was in the habit of taking his music with him when he fed the hens.

"Lord, yes!" said Max. "He never puts the damn thing down."

"Ah," said Virgil. "I would hazard a guess that therein lies your problem."

"How so?"

"I can't pretend to any knowledge of hens and their husbandry. But if my body were being jarred by the sounds of Johnny Retch and the Bleeding Zits, I think I'd feel invaded. I can't somehow imagine that I would be able to lay an egg, or do anything that was creative and life affirming. Who knows? Maybe if you were to play those songs backward, they would contain all kinds of messages that are inimical to hens. If I were you, Max, I'd ask Jeremy to can the music around the coop, and see if that makes a difference."

Both Max and I felt that Virgil was perhaps ascribing too great a power to music, and said as much.

"It makes sense, though," he insisted. "Music both soothes and agitates. It's powerful stuff. Try it, Max. What have you got to lose?"

Sometimes, Virgil's ideas are impossibly far fetched. He's come up with some lulus over time. But every so often, he astonishes me with his insight and acuity. This was just such an instance. Within two days of a ban being issued on the playing of heavy metal music in the hen yard, the eggs were once again rolling like Jordan.

Was it Shakespeare who said that every action has an equal and opposite reaction? Probably not. In any case, Max is using that principle as the basis of an experiment. He reasoned that if loud and obnoxious music is an impediment to egg production, then the introduction of soothing melodies might make the hens even more fecund. Virgil is enthusiastic in his support of this research. He gave Max a tape of *The Four Seasons* to play for his brood, and while this has not led to an appreciable increase in laying, Max claims that his clucking charges are grinning from ear to ear.

"I didn't think chickens could grin," I remarked to Virgil.

"I didn't think they had ears," he answered. "I wonder if they would appreciate bassoon music? Mrs. Rochester certainly does."

And so, all this quiet September afternoon, while the rest of the house is in recovery, Virgil has stood in the pantry with Mrs. Rochester as his small but appreciative audience, recording gentle tunes for the benefit of Max's chickens. "The Swan" by Saint Saëns. The Newfoundland folk song, "She's Like the Swallow." His own solo bassoon arrangement of the Pachelbel "Canon." Sweet, sad songs that are so well suited both to the day and to this season of slow rot.

From where I sit, I can look out at our small garden, at the sweet peas and snapdragons and zinnias. They are having their last hurrah. Our single pear tree is in a rather sorry state of neglect. We have not made much use of its gifts this year. I note that the wasps have attained that state of addled stupidity that comes over them in their old age. They are rolling about on the pungent scatter of windfall fruit, revelling in the felicitous ooze of our poor pears. I wonder if they will wake up tomorrow with hangovers?

When Altona stopped by this morning and found me in the throes of boozy aftermath, she brought over the latest copy of the *Rumor* and hinted broadly that I pay special attention to the horoscopes, for which she is responsible. She took on this responsibility after completing a correspondence course in astrology.

"Go easy over these next few weeks, Taurus. You are coming to the end of a period of intense activity. Now the heat's off, you can get out of the kitchen. You owe it to yourself to take a breather. A change of scene would do you a world of good! Why not take a little holiday with a loved one? You've worked hard. It's time to have a bit of fun!"

For some time, Altona has been suggesting that we should take a holiday together. I have no objection to this. In fact, I think it is a good idea, especially since the stars are conspiring to bring it about. But regardless of heaven's will, holidays will have to wait for a while yet. The summer storm has blown over, but the dust has far from settled.

My stomach, on the other hand, is quite settled now, much to my relief. I attribute this to the healing qualities of mint tea. My tea ball appears to have come apart in the pot, as the cup I have just poured is full of floating leaves. I'll drain the liquid and ask Virgil to have a look at the residue. He claims a certain skill at teacup reading. Is it possible that the future can be contained in a random scattering of leaves? Or stars? Or palmar lines? Who is to say? ♠

Beth

Every summer, I make a real conscientious effort to do something I've never done before. Last year, I went for a ride in a hot air balloon. The year before, I went to recorder camp. The year before that, I took courses in spinning and making natural dyes. These summertime interests are like summertime romances. It's not important to pursue them once the season is done. I suppose that Jane Austen is my only hot weather flirtation to have blossomed into an enduring passion.

I read my first Jane Austen—*Emma*—the summer after I turned sixteen. That was a summer of many firsts. It was the summer of my first job. It was the summer I became the first girl ever employed as a dishwasher at the Brigadoon Beach Resort Hotel. And it was the summer I became the first Jew ever to work there in any capacity.

Lois got me the job. She was my best—in fact, my only—friend. It was one of those peculiar unions, based largely on the fact that we were both misfits. We were the weird girls. I was marginally weird because I was Jewish and perceived to be brainy in a school that was waspy and athletic. Lois was really weird. She was a crusader for civil rights. She circulated petitions protesting the Vietnam war. She was suspended for a week because she wore jeans in contravention of the dress code. She wrote poetry and cultivated dark circles under her eyes. She organized coffee houses in local church basements. She played the guitar, after a fashion, and sang high, lilting ballads in the style of Joan Baez, whom she revered.

Lois's Auntie Doris ran Brigadoon. She had inherited the business from her fifth husband, Ted. Ted had bad valves and died scarcely a month after the wedding. Auntie Doris was used to mates coming and going, but this was too much even for her. His unscheduled departure left her feeling tired out. She was too bewildered by bereavement and too self-absorbed to pay much mind to the unwritten but rigid conventions of the place. One of these was that a woman's place was in the cocktail lounge or in the front of the coffee house, and not in the kitchen. The other was that Jews belonged on the other side of the lake, at Alexandra Beach. This sounds so shameful now. It was shameful then, to be sure. But it was a long-established tradition, respected and upheld as rigorously by Jews as by Gentiles.

"Why would you want to go where you're not wanted?" was my mother's sensible question, when I asked her if I might spend the summer with Lois, working at Brigadoon.

"For one thing, it's a job. And besides, this kind of segregation is ridiculous. This is no different from Alabama. Or Georgia. This is just like a colour bar, and somebody's got to be the first to break it."

I am not now, and I was not then, a trailblazer for social justice. And even though I truly believed all this, I recognized Lois's words coming out of my mouth. It was exactly what she would have said.

We had had many late-night discussions about racial and religious intolerance. The long tradition of quiet anti-Semitism at Brigadoon made her bile rise. While I'm sure she went to bat for me with Auntie Doris because she liked me and wanted a friend around for the summer, I'm also sure she interceded on my behalf because it satisfied her reformer impulse.

My mother heard me out and then just shrugged. She was tired out, too. After years of bickering, she and my father had decided to go their separate ways, and she had no more fight left in her.

"So go," were her final words to him and me, both.

I don't know if I would have gone to Brigadoon had I understood I would be bussing tables and washing dishes at the Rainbow's End Coffee Shop. Lois had led me to expect we would be waitressing together. That, she told me, was the arrangement she had worked out with her aunt. But somehow, the grieving Doris had suppressed the knowledge I would be tagging along, and my arrival took her by surprise. Lois completed her required complement of servers. She simply did not need another waitress. But one of the kitchen helpers had been laid low by a persistent case of mononucleosis. He would be out for the rest of the summer. The job was mine if I wanted it. Otherwise, I would have to return home.

"How bad can it be?" asked Lois. "At least we'll get to work the same shifts. And I'll split my tips with you."

So I signed on.

My job was not glamorous. As soon as a party left a table, I swooped down like an avenging angel. I removed the dishes to a malodorous grey basin that I wheeled about on an awkward trolley. I wiped the arborite clear of the crumby detritus. Then I gave the surface a once over with filthy cloth, doused with vinegar. I wheeled the dishes into the kitchen and scraped them of their worst remains. Then I loaded them into a dark, satanic dishwasher. It rumbled and belched clouds of scalding steam whenever its jaws were pried apart. Often it would go berserk and grind up all its passengers into porcelain shards.

Whenever this happened—and it happened with great regularity—Willi would be summoned to put things right. Willi was the resort handyman. He would spend hours tinkering with the thing, muttering low, Polish curses, while the dishes piled up. Finally, he

117

would pronounce the machine repaired, and it would belch and rattle on for another day or two before committing some new atrocity.

I was not welcome in Willi's world. In fact, he hated me on sight. It was an uncluttered kind of hatred, unalloyed, and almost admirable in its simplicity. He hated me for being female, and he hated me for being a Jew. I don't know how he guessed I was Jewish. I didn't call attention to the fact. Nor, thankfully, did Lois. She seemed satisfied to have played a pivotal role in breaking the long embargo and didn't feel the need to harp on her accomplishment. My family name—Brown—betrayed nothing. And I was decidedly Aryan in my appearance. I didn't "look" Jewish, at least not in the way that I imagine Willi would have understood "looking Jewish." Nevertheless, he knew. He intuited it, somehow. He didn't like it one little bit, and he made sure I knew.

Early on that summer, on one of the many afternoons the dishwasher was engaged in a work stoppage, I made the mistake of wondering out loud why the superannuated and recalcitrant machine simply wasn't replaced. Willi, who was deep in its guts at the time, reared up and snarled, "If I say it can be fixed, it can be fixed. So shut up, smart little know-it-all Jew. Know who you are around here? No one. You're no one."

Where does such a hot, pure hatred begin? I don't know. But it commands a certain respect. And his rude summation of the pecking order was undeniably accurate. At Brigadoon, I was indeed no one. The lowest of the low. My every task brought me into contact with other people's unpleasant remains. Congealing egg yolk. Mounded chips, slathered with ketchup and gravy. Unappealing crusts. Bits of discarded hamburger, all marked with the crescent-shape scars left by incisors. If someone was ill, it was my job to clean up the mess. I even had to clean the men's washroom, to remove the cigarette butts from the urinals and swab the ugly toilets.

"Oh God, I'm so sorry," Lois would say from time to time, when she saw me about to embark on another awful chore.

But as time went on, I cultivated a kind of easygoing attitude about it all. I was enjoying being away from home, enjoying the freedom to create myself in my own image. I was surprised that I had the physical resources to do the work, surprised I had the psychic wherewithal to carry on in what was often a hostile environment. Not only did I have to contend with Willi. There was Joe.

Joe couldn't have been more than twenty, but he seemed old and dangerous. He was thin and weedy, with sallow skin and sparse hair and a moustache that sat on his lip like a nervous cockroach. Joe was a cook at Rainbow's End. It was well known he was "getting it on" with Wendy, who was a hostess at the coffee shop. He had many tales to tell of their highly athletic lovemaking and would point to his bruised neck as evidence of their mutual exertions. Between orders, Joe would sit on a milk crate and tell dirty stories. He would speculate uncharitably on the private lives of our coworkers and would eventually turn his grotesque beacon on me. I ignored his harangue and simply continued to scrape dishes and load the washer. Once, this became too much for him. He came up behind me, groped for my breasts, and whispered in a voice that was meant to be seductive and full of meaning, "You like that, don't you?"

Some of my memories of that summer of firsts are vivid post cards. I have such a clear picture of Joe's astonished face as, in a single motion, I turned around, smashed the plate I was holding, and pointed a scythe-shaped shard in the general direction of his throat. Nothing was said. There was no need for words. In that moment, I understood so much. I understood how hatred like Willi's was possible. I understood that I had it in me, not so very far beneath the surface, to inflict serious damage on another person. I understood that there are times when a certain ruthlessness is not necessarily a bad thing. And I understood that Joe would never bother me again.

Overall, it was a summer of learning. I learned, finally, how to load the dishwasher with the skill and delicate panache of a croupier dealing cards at blackjack. I learned how to fool Doris into thinking a floor was cleaner than it was by using more ammonia than was necessary. I learned that human flesh can turn blue in the space of thirty seconds and that I could rise to the occasion in an emergency. A guest swallowed an inadequately chewed home fry potato. He reared up in his seat, snorting like a stallion. He went from red, to white, to blue, rather like the flag of France.

A hushed fascination fell over the Rainbow's End.

I do not think we had ever been taught the Heimlich manoeuvre in hygiene class. I'm not entirely sure that Heimlich had even made his great discovery. But somehow, I knew instinctively what to do. I grabbed the man around his middle and gave a hearty squeeze. The potato rose from his gullet and flew from his mouth, its impressive trajectory carrying it clear across the room, where it landed, most incredibly of all, in the open cash register. Never have I believed so deeply in the existence of God. There was a small scattering of applause. The man tried to press some money onto me, but I demurred. Then I went back to washing dishes.

At the end of the day, neither Lois nor I had much energy for anything but gossiping and reading. In our shared cabin there was a small bookcase filled with the reading material left behind by our predecessors at Brigadoon: mostly romances and detective stories and Reader's Digest condensed novels. These we devoured. There were a few more challenging titles, too. *Lolita,* I remember, and *The Robe.* But it was *Emma* that touched me deepest. *Emma* was the right book at the right time: a story of spiritual progress, of quiet humour, of love and growing. Its combination of upheaval and quiet certainty was exactly what I required during that summer when everything around me was changing so quickly, and my childhood was forsaking me, thundering away like a speeding locomotive. I read *Emma* three times that summer, and when I returned home at the end of August, I raided the library for *Pride and Prejudice* and *Persuasion* and *Mansfield Park* and *Northanger Abbey.* I came to love Jane Austen's still, quiet, ironic voice. I have never tired of it, and there are not many things in a life that endure so shiningly.

Whenever I read Austen—*Emma,* most particularly—I remember Brigadoon Beach and that summer of firsts. I have thought of it often during this stay at your bed and breakfast, particularly as I have watched our plates being removed from the table, all sticky with egg yolk and dotted with toast crumbs. A real dishwashing challenge. Sometimes, I have felt a kind of itching in my palms, a surprising eagerness to get into the kitchen, pick up a brillo pad, and just scrub away for old time's sake. You will have noticed that I resisted the urge, however. I suppose you could call this an instance when sense won out over sensibility.

Thanks for your hospitality. Thanks for having HP Sauce on the table. And the eggs, if messy, were always delicious. ♠

Grace Abounding

People who find their way to our valley and stay here for a short while; or who hear about it from friends; or who read about it in accounts such as these, might well think that we inhabit a kind of latter day Shangri-la: a bucolic, pastoral paradise, charming and backward, untouched and untrivialized by the grotesqueries of our time. In some respects, they are not far wrong. Those who have chosen to come here to live, and we who have chosen never to leave, are largely of a single mind when it comes to considerations of "quality of life." We like things slow, and we like things simple.

This is not to say that we are insular in any way. I hope we are not blinkered and backward, or provincial and hostile to outside influences. What is good and new we embrace wholeheartedly. The introduction of an espresso machine to the Well of Loneliness was widely applauded. And no one winced when the lambada finally found its way into our occasional community dances. But every so often there are less appealing incursions; and while we might wish there were some way we could insulate ourselves from the sad delinquencies that sometimes blow our way from the great beyond, we must acknowledge that such a thing is, alas, not possible. We are part of the world, after all, and it is a world rife with troubles. Perhaps those rare instances of sociopathic display that sometimes ripple the calm surface of this place should be seen as necessary and useful reminders of how fortunate we are. We have just had such an occurrence.

"VANDALS DECAPITATE MAILBOXES" blared the headline in yesterday's hastily produced edition of the *Occasional Rumor*. It was a bizarre and senseless incident. Most of us have—or rather, had—country-style mailboxes at the foot of our drives. Each was a piece of folk art. Ours was a lovely wooden rectangle, painted a bright yellow. Rainbows described an arc along its length on either side, and the flag that was raised to signal occupancy was a bright red. During the night, some perverse squad travelled up and down our road, removing a dozen or more letter receptacles from their posts and making off with them.

"Who would do such a thing?" I mused to Hector.

"A rogue band of curio dealers, I suppose," he said. "Probably they'll wind up in antique stores in Vancouver and fetch hundreds of dollars apiece as examples of naive primitivism. It's too bad. I'll miss the old thing. Not that it was good for much."

This was true. The kidnapped boxes were strictly decorative and served no real functional purpose: home delivery of the mail stopped here some years back, as part of a misguided cost-saving measure on the part of the post office. Now, we retrieve our letters and parcels from a "community mailbox" in the village. This means that we must walk almost a mile to collect our mail, which is a bit of a nuisance when the weather is foul or when the B & B pace is frantic. However, it does provide one of us with the excuse for a head-clearing stroll; and the pickup point is within spitting distance of the Well of Loneliness and its potent coffees.

I was there only this morning, punctuating my perusal of the mail with sips of a frothy cappuccino.

"Anything of note?" bellowed June over the hiss of the milk steamer. She and Rae joined me at my table.

"The usual, for the most part. Bills, receipts, statements, a reservation or two, another letter from the *Reader's Digest* letting me know I might already have won a million dollars."

"You subscribe to the *Reader's Digest*?" asked Rae.

"Mother did," I said, with a faint and unnecessary tone of apology. I don't know why it's so fashionable to sneer at the *Reader's Digest*. I've learned a great deal from it over the years about the function of the major organs, and how to keep love alive in a marriage. "We've kept up the subscription as a kind of memorial. And anyway, I rather like it. Great toilet- side reading. Ah! And here's Hector's copy of *Conjurer's Monthly*. Just in time for Thanksgiving. He'll be pleased."

"*Conjurer's Monthly*?" asked June. "For Hector? I had no idea! Does he sneak into your room at night and try to saw you in half?"

"Better have another cappuccino, then," said Rae. "You'll want to stay awake. Is this a hobby of long standing with Hector? Or a recent interest?"

Their ferreting instincts had been aroused. Once the milk steamer had accomplished its loud task and the thick brew with its choco-late-dotted foam was set before me, I launched in.

When we decided to open our home as a bed and breakfast, there was only one practicality that worried us. While we knew that the work would be absorbing and require our full attention, we neither of us wanted to be devoured by a monster of our own making. We wanted some semblance of a private life and didn't care to find that we were expected to be camp counsellors or short-order cooks. We decided to encourage a sense of "make yourself to home" self-suffi-ciency among our guests and to limit our culinary obligations to preparing and serving breakfast.

"After all," Hector pointed out, "we're not calling ourselves The Bachelor Brothers' Bed and Three Squares a Day."

This was some years before June and Rae opened the Well, and as there was no other restaurant or café in the near vicinity, it was evident that the only way our visitors could sidestep starva-tion would be if they had free and open access to our kitchen. At first glance, you might think this would be a logistical nightmare; and I confess that at first I was more than a little leery about the prospect of eight strangers vying for a home on the range and staking out claims in the cold white confines of the fridge. It is not, as it turns out, an arrangement that suits everybody. But others find the prospect intriguing, and as we explain the situa-tion very carefully to first-timers, we have rarely had to deal with hungry whiners.

A few of our visitors—very few, actually—keep to themselves at mealtimes, as they have every right to do. They prepare the food they have brought or purchased from the little market in the village and find a quiet place to eat and read. Some, now that it is a possibility, choose to dine at the Well of Loneliness: at least, on those several days a week that June and Rae deign to open the doors. But for the most part, a genial conviviality settles over the group, and without our suggesting it or arranging it in any way, lunches and suppers turn into friendly and sometimes expansive potlucks in which everyone plays a part. Some are very enthusiastic, indeed. There are always those who spend much more of their time reading Julia Child or Elizabeth David than Iris Murdoch or Toni Morrison: a choice, freely made, which works to the benefit of the company. Hector and I sometimes join in, depending on the vagaries of scheduling and mood. I always enjoy watching people who are strangers getting to know one another. There is something about chewing in the company of others that breaks down that edge of *froideur* with which most us shield ourselves.

It occurs to me that most animals like to eat in groups. You can see city crows doing their seriocomic alleyway dance around the chicken bones and clamshells they've pulled from the tangle of a restaurant garbage bin. Watch a nature documentary about a pride of lions, contented in the Serengeti sun, lying around the chewed over carcass of a zebra. Go to a Chinese restaurant (how I wish there were one in our valley!) and watch friends and families sparring verbally and with chopsticks over *dim sum*.

We are not so very far removed from the impulse that makes crows and lions and other creatures choose to dine with likeminded others. But because we are human and feel that Nature can be perked up by forcing a tablespoon or two of Art down her throat, we have added various refinements to the communal process: flatware, napkins, tablecloths, tipping. Another of the traits that distinguishes Us from the winged and finned and four-footed Them is that we can ostensibly look beyond ourselves and speculate that we owe a debt of something like gratitude to a force or power that is grander than ourselves. At the dinner table, this consciousness is sometimes formalized and articulated by way of saying a blessing, or grace. It's an old, old custom. Thousands of years ago, the writer of Deuteronomy counselled, "Thou shalt eat and be satisfied and bless the Lord thy God for the good land which He has given thee." I have never made a formal study of the subject, but I would be willing to speculate that every culture in every age has had a tradition of honouring that which is about to be consumed by saying a few words of thanks.

In our own time, at least in the Western world, I think it is a habit or formality that has largely been discarded. Saying grace was never a part of our growing up, since Mother was a convinced atheist. As a child, I was once deeply embarrassed when I was invited to eat at someone else's home and was asked to pronounce a preprandial blessing. I hadn't the faintest idea what to say. None of the formulas lived in my head. Not "God is great, God is good, let us thank him for our food." Not "For that which we are about to receive, may the Lord make us truly thankful." Not even the blasphemous "Good food, good meat, good God, let's eat."

I had repressed this incident until last Thanksgiving. The house, as is usually the case on long weekends, was operating to capacity, and our guests—all of them regulars—had come prepared to make the Sunday evening meal a memorable one. A dozen people sat around a board that groaned under the weight of antipasto, smoked mussels, oysters on the half shell, lox, pâtés, cheeses, French bread, steaming casseroles populated with yam soufflé, mustard-glazed carrots, squash and apple compote, peas, and potatoes in various incarnations. Hector, Altona, and I took responsibility for the turkey and its stuffing: a cunning amalgam of corn, red pepper, and toasted almonds. Wines and liqueurs stood in their ranks. No stop had been left unpulled.

We sat down, appreciative murmurs on every lip, and lost no time tucking in. The conversation turned this way and that, and it wasn't until we had almost all cleared our plates and were beginning to think about the possibility of seconds that one woman said, "Oh, dear! We forgot to say grace!"

"Grace?" said the man on her right. "I can't remember the last time I said grace."

"I don't think I actually know one."

"We never said it when I was growing up."

"We might have, at Christmas and Thanksgiving. I can't quite remember."

"We said it at camp. The only one I remember was 'Rub a dub dub, let's get to the grub.'"

"We said it all the time. My father was a minister. It used to make me crazy, having to sit there and smell the food while he droned on. I'd sneak bites while everyone else's eyes were closed. I guess I was a pretty revolting creature."

I told my sad story, and said, "It's rather a nice idea, though. Grace, I mean. It wouldn't hurt any of us to acknowledge how lucky we are."

"There's no reason we can't do that now," said Peggy, the woman who first noted we had been remiss. "Everyone here has something to be grateful for. We could each say a few words."

"A *very* few words," added cynical Michael, the preacher's son.

And that is what we did. We went round the table, each of listening to the others say a few words of thanks.

"For friends."

"For being here."

"For all this bounty."

"For the word."

"For the flesh."

"For joy and sorrow, pleasure and pain."

"For love, given and received."

Michael, the disaffected son of a minister, was the last to speak. His words: "For earth, for water, for air, and for fire." Then he did the most remarkable thing. He took his linen table napkin and held it up for everyone to see. We watched him fold it into the shape of a thick wick, watched him thrust it into the candle flame. We were too astonished to speak or to move, too surprised and mesmerized by this bizarre and unexpected action to even process the data and make sense of it. He held the napkin aloft in his right hand while the fire took hold. Then—strangest of all—he pulled the improvised torch through his clenched left fist, never wincing, and once again held the napkin up for inspection. There was no fire, no smoke, no smell of burning. And when he unfurled it, with a flourish, it was intact, unscorched, free of holes or burn marks. He placed it back in his lap, raised his glass to the room and said, "Thanks, too, for magic."

To say we were amazed would be to understate the case. And Altona, who had inherited the napkins from her grandmother, was nearly apoplectic. Hector, though, who sat on the magician's left, was thrilled.

"How did you do that?" he demanded.

"Like this," said Michael. He reached into Hector's ear and extracted an egg. "You can poach this in the morning."

You could have knocked anyone at the table over with a feather. And Hector was over the moon with excitement.

"How? How?" he pleaded, but to no avail. The wizard kept his counsel. He did volunteer, however, that he was the editor of a newsletter aimed at sleight-of-hand enthusiasts, both professionals and gifted amateurs, and that he would be pleased to give Hector a complimentary year's subscription.

"As a gift of thanksgiving, for your kindnesses."

"Will you publish the napkin trick?"

"Perhaps," was as committed an answer as Michael was willing to give.

To date, it has not appeared, and Hector's gift subscription runs out with this most recent issue.

"So this is the last chance," said June, when I had told the story.

"What's he learned so far?" asked Rae.

"Oh, a few tricks with cards and coins. He can pull the Queen of Hearts out of any deck and make a quarter disappear from the left hand and show up in the right. But it's the flaming napkin he's waiting for."

"Altona will be thrilled," said June. "I hope he practises with paper serviettes first."

"And outside," added her partner. "By the way, is Michael going to be with you again this Thanksgiving?"

"No. We haven't heard from him."

"Too bad. I thought perhaps he could make the mailboxes reappear."

Hector's *Conjurer's Monthly* was sealed. I couldn't look at the contents to see if we were likely to be treated to a display of pyrotechnics. Just in case, I stopped at Abel Wackaugh's to pick up another small fire extinguisher. I will leave it on his bed, along with the newsletter. I walked home, buzzing a little with the caffeine, taking sad note of the dozen or so naked posts where the boxes once sat. I think it unlikely we will ever see them again. And in a few months, no one will remember they were there. This is the way of the world, my friends: the strange and magical troubled world. ♠

A Poem by Solomon Solomon

The Tiger Says Grace

Dear God who cares for tigers,
I have much to thank you for.
My stripes and leafy jungle home,
My throaty purr, my roar.
I thank you for the blazing sun,
And for the cooling shower,
And for the tasty hunter
I'm preparing to devour.
Dear God you have been generous
To send this meaty one,
Encumbered by nearsightedness
And by a faulty gun.
Oh, he was easy prey to stalk!
A most unequal match!
I leapt on him with claws unsheathed
And slew with quick dispatch.
So now he lies before me
With his dim, unseeing eyes,
His face bedecked with nothing
But a look of slight surprise.
And do I feel remorse's pull?
No. Not one guilty tug.
It's better he should be my lunch
Than I should be his rug.
So, God who cares for tigers
And who made us burning bright,
Thank you for your kindness,
I'll sleep happily tonight. ♙

Tired and Feathered

Praise be, we have come to the end of a beautiful day. A day that was all the lovelier for being unexpected. A day that was a perfect pearl pulled from the bland, grey oyster we call November. For the last week, the sun has been hiding its light under a cloudy bushel. Today, it decided to come out for one last hurrah. We all joined the chorus. "Hurrah!" we cried, as we stepped into its warm, obliquely angled light. "Hip hip hooray!" we shouted, breathing in that sweet, autumnal smell of rot, that potpourri made of leaf mould and the sad exhalations of drowsy, naked trees.

This was not a day made for discouraging words. "Yes!" was on every lip, and every mind was enlivened by the thrilling knowledge that while winter was grinding his old, familiar axe, we had been granted a short reprieve, a day's stay of execution.

The times were pleasantly out of joint, and anomalous behaviour seemed the order of the day. My melancholy brother forsook his pantry practice room and took his bassoon onto the porch, where he played "Flight of the Bumblebee." Darlene and Susan hung a "Gone Fishing" sign on the Rubyfruit Jungle. J. MacDonald Bellweather wore his kilt when he went to pick up a string of digitalized Christmas lights he had ordered through Abel Wackaugh. This was reported to me by Altona, when she pulled up to the house in her recently acquired four wheel–drive van. Her little dog, Valentine, was grinning on the seat beside her, his Pekingese eyes bulging from his unfortunate face. I can't look at Valentine without thinking about plastic surgery, although I've learned to stifle the impulse to say so. At least around Altona.

"This is the day the Lord has made, and he made it for long walks with dogs," she said. "Can you get away?"

I didn't see why not. Our three guests had been watered and fed, and seemed content when last sighted. There was no chore so pressing that it couldn't bear the weight of a slight delay. So I stuck my odour eaters in my sneakers, grabbed a couple of granola bars and a bag of trail mix, and away we went. En route, we picked up June and Rae and their doddering golden retriever, Toklas. Then we headed for the cemetery.

Altona was not alone in her inspiration. I would guess that every dog owner in the valley had the same idea. They were everywhere. Big dogs, small dogs, old dogs, young dogs, white dogs, black dogs, tan dogs, spotted dogs, dogs of distinguished pedigree, and goofy SPCA rescue mutts of low degree. Dogs of every persuasion charged around the graveyard, playing their games of tag under the trees, around the stones, and above the stiffs who lay beneath. They greeted each other in their genial, courtly way, snuffling and licking. They would come together in packs, then spread out, helter skelter, like a blob of mercury.

"Isn't it amazing," said June, as she watched old Toklas sniff the bottom of a youthful Dalmatian, "that they almost never fight. Every now and then one snaps or growls, but it never goes anywhere."

"What is there to fight about?" asked Altona. "None of them has religion. None of them wants to annex territory. They don't want to call each other names. They don't hanker after anything except to go on being a dog. They're happy just to pee all over everything and have a good time."

"They seem to have it figured out," I agreed. "I think we should give them a chance at running the world."

"Good idea! A government of dogs," said Rae. "Like Chaucer's Parliament of Fowls. It would be difficult to arrange, though. Maybe we should keep the same world leaders but make them take a lesson from dogs. We could strip them all naked and turn them loose in a park. They could sniff each other and run around until they were too tired out to make a fuss."

I tried to imagine such a scene but found myself stifling a gag reflex. We fell into a companionable silence. We sat on a bench, four in a row, sunning ourselves like lizards on a rock. We passed the trail mix back and forth, thinking our separate thoughts. I wondered where we went wrong, as a species, that we seem so bent on liberating the blood from each other's veins. Other animals are so peaceable. Oh sure, they sometimes do each other in. But it's always a function of instinct rather than malice. And they never go in for mass slaughter with cruel and invented weapons. For the most part, they inhabit a peaceable kingdom. Even those creatures that are supposed to be sworn enemies—dogs and cats, cats and birds—very often get along.

Dogs are welcome in our home, and we never worry about Waffle. Visiting puppies somehow understand that she belongs, that she is a fixture of the place, and not to be troubled or disturbed. We rarely see an instance of canine-feline conflict; which is all to the good, as Waffle is superbly skilled in paw-to-paw combat and shows no mercy when riled. One good clout to the snout is all it takes to put a marauding mastiff in his place. Although it is true that our calico likes to play Diana the Huntress and wrap her lips around a careless wren or sparrow that might let down its guard in the garden, she has never so much as licked her chops around Mrs. Rochester.

Our guests and visitors are often surprised to find we have both a cat and a bird in residence. They suppose the parrot must be forever looking over her shoulder, fearful that Waffle is nearby and dreaming of drumsticks. Not so. From the very day of Waffle's "over the transom" arrival till now, they have accorded one another the space and latitude each requires to play out her role, both in the household and in the world. I don't know if they could properly be called "friends," as they tend to regard one another cordially and from a distance. That is, until November comes along. Then, their relationship takes on a different cast, and they become enthusiastic co-operators.

This is the time of year when it occurs to mice to seek pastures that may not be green but are at least warm and dry. Year after year, they take the advice of some misguided Moses, who points out our house and says: "Lo! Before you stands a veritable land of milk and honey! A Club Med for you and all your children. Pack your bags! Move on in!" And they do.

Every November, we find the evidence of their efforts to colonize. The droppings. Corners gnawed from bags of flour. Sidelong glimpses of something fast and furry, scurrying. Nighttime sounds of tiny feet, scuttling. Unhappily for them, and luckily for us, we have the world's most effective mouse control agency: Mrs. Rochester and Waffle, working in tandem. They are a miraculous force, an incredible blending of talents. Mrs. Rochester sits on her perch in the kitchen, doing her little jig and keeping a sharp eye out for any sign of aberrant activity. The second she sees anything that looks even remotely suspicious, she summons her cohort with a bell-like cry: "He - e - e - e - e - r - r - r - e kittykittykittykitty! Pusspusspuss!" Waffle arrives with the speed and assurance of a ballistic missile and dispatches the offender while Mrs. Rochester looks on, cackling and delighted, like an old duenna at a bullfight.

This goes on for a couple of weeks, until finally the point is driven home and the decimated ranks of rodents migrate elsewhere. I would like it better if we could all just sit down and negotiate a treaty, or come to some understanding. But as such a thing is not possible, I am thankful for this partnership; this living, organic mousetrap; this union of nature and art that spares us the awful necessity of turning to the technology of extinction: Setting traps. Laying poison.

The only disadvantage to this creative union is that we are not always able to supervise the disposition of the remains of their victims. Sometimes, we find corpses in unexpected places. For instance, just last night I discovered the remnants of rodents inside our jack-o'-lantern. Hallowe'en was two weeks ago, and the artfully carved pumpkin has been on the porch all that time, its face falling in on itself, bits of mould starting to show here and there. I am reluctant, always, to dispose of the trappings of any season. If I had my way, I'd leave the Christmas tree up until Easter. It's my brother—ruthless, orderly and wedded to the idea that to everything there is a season and that seasons are of limited duration—who stands in the way of this. I would certainly have let our ghostly lantern sit a while longer, had Virgil not seen me taking some vegetable parings and eggshells out to our garden compost pile.

"Would you mind adding the jack-o'-lantern to that load?" he asked. "It's starting to smell just a little high."

He was right. In fact, it was stinkier than it ought to have been, given that it was outside, in the cool and preserving autumn air. Sadly, I stopped on the stoop and bent to scoop. I peered through the pumpkin's eyes, looked into its hollow, malodorous head—like Hamlet examining Yorick—and found I was staring at the stiffened remnants of not one but half a dozen mice. No wonder it was the source of such olfactory unpleasantness. It was not a happy way to usher out the Hallowe'en season. But perhaps it was an apt period to place at the end of the sentence, given what happened to us on Hallowe'en itself.

We do not very often leave the valley for social occasions. It's not that we're reclusive or hermetic in any way. We're just busy. However, Altona—who is forever trying to broaden our horizons—had got wind of a Hallowe'en dance and potluck supper being sponsored by an island service club in a community hall just over the hills.

"What do you think?" she asked one morning, as we were all three of us having coffee in the kitchen.

"Sounds fine," I said.

"You two young people go out and have a good time," said Virgil. "I can stay here and hold down the fort."

Altona clucked. "Virgil! Don't be such a stick-in-the-mud. You never get out. Let's go as a threesome. Me and my two men. Every other woman in the place will be fit to be tied. I'll take that spicy Thai noodle salad. Everyone likes it."

I saw Virgil recoil just slightly at this news. The last time he ate Altona's spicy Thai noodle salad, he had an unhappy encounter with a pepper that resonated for days. Still, he was pleased to be included in the evening and said so.

"What will you boys bring along?"

"Perhaps," said Virgil, "we could bring some caramel-covered apples. They're easy enough to make ahead of time and right for the season."

"Perfect!" said Altona. "And don't you worry about the costumes. I'll take care of everything!"

On the afternoon of the party, true to her word, Altona appeared with two of the most remarkable get-ups I have ever seen. I would never have thought that such things could be created by mortal hands. As we donned them, she explained how she had spent hours at a stretch culling discarded feathers from Max Janzen's hens and from every other chicken coop in the district.

"Bags of them! Bags and bags!"

These she had taken home and applied, painstakingly, with some miraculous adhesive, to coveralls and to balaclavas. She had made beaks from paper cups, and crowns from egg cartons, and stitched these to the headgear. We slipped everything on and stood before a full-length mirror: two very convincing roosters. I didn't know whether to laugh or sneeze, so I just whistled, admiringly.

"You'll see mine tonight! You won't believe it!" she crowed. "Pick me up at seven! Toodle-oo!"

"I can hardly wait," muttered Virgil. "Perhaps I'll go start the candied apples."

We can neither of us remember how long we have had our electric range. Forever just about sums it up. It is simple and reliable, and all we have ever wanted or needed. We have never given in to the seductive siren whispers of microwaves or convection ovens. We don't even have a toaster oven. Why our dependable Moffat decided to pack it in on this very day is anyone's guess. The fact is that it simply could not be encouraged to produce heat, not by any coaxing, and we were left without a means of melting the caramels in which we meant to dip our potluck apples.

As it happened, though, Altona and I had watched a fascinating report on a late-night talk show about something called "manifold cookery." It's a very straightforward idea. You strap some raw foodstuff to the manifold of your car. Then you drive a certain distance, and the heat from the engine cooks it. The man on the talk show had driven a distance of two hundred miles and presented the host with a slab of steak, medium rare, which he had prepared in this way.

The community hall in question is at a distance of forty miles.

"Surely that will be enough to melt a few caramels," I said to Virgil, when I suggested to him that this might be a solution to our dilemma.

"Oh no. No. I don't think so. I'll just give Abel a call, and he'll come by to fix it."

"Abel won't get here until six, and by that time it will be too late."

"Then perhaps we should just stop on the way for some chips and dip."

"Don't be such a chicken!" I said, scarcely pausing to consider the irony of this remark. "What harm can it do?"

And so it was that before we set out to retrieve Altona, we donned our costumes, filled a pot with caramels, and waddled out to our old pickup. We opened the hood and stared into the labyrinth.

"And what, precisely, is the manifold?" asked Virgil, his words slightly muffled by his feathery balaclava.

"Beats me," I answered. "But it seems to fit here."

I wedged the pot in between a couple of hoses that looked like they had the potential to become quite warm. It seemed very secure. We slammed the hood shut, fired up the truck *cum* oven, and with Virgil at the wheel, we drove the several miles to Altona's.

Wasn't she a vision! She too was covered in feathers: but hers had been attached to what I believe is called a "bustier" or "merry widow." She looked like something out of an illustrated mythology, one of those hybrid creatures, half-woman, half-poultry.

"My God," said Virgil, as she strutted out to the truck.

Altona sat between us and gave us each a peck (and I do mean a peck) on the cheek. She brushed off our compliments with a glib wave of her hand. A few feathers came unglued and drifted into the Thai noodle salad she clutched on her lap. We pointed our truck in the direction of the hall and said "Giddyup."

"My smart boys!" said Altona, when we told her that we were melting caramels even as we drove. Over the hills we bounced, over the hills and far away. It was quite a jouncy ride, given the parlous state of our suspension and the pockmarked roads. But we were merry and full of the anticipation of fun. When we had gone thirty of the forty miles, Virgil pulled to the side, and I opened the hood to see how the caramels were coming along.

"They're soft," I reported, "but not melted yet. If we take the long way and add another ten miles, they should be ready for dipping by the time we arrive."

"Fine with me," said Altona.

"Right you are," said Virgil.

The long way is a glorified logging route that is even more rutted and pothole-ridden than the road we were on. Our poor truck laboured, but we didn't mind. The hotter the engine, the faster we would achieve the desired liquefaction. I think the caramels must have reached meltdown at exactly the moment we thudded into a crater that might have been left by an errant meteor. It was a bladder-and-bowel-shaking drop. Of course, I could not see what was happening under the hood; but I can only imagine that the pot was jarred from its moorings, spilling its sticky contents all over the throbbing heart of the machine. It gave a rasping, choking sound, and shuddered into silence.

It was quite dark. We three sat and looked out into the night.

"How far are we from the hall?" asked Altona, her teeth just slightly clenched.

"Oh—five, maybe six miles," said Virgil.

"Nice night for a walk," she said.

"I don't know quite what else we can do," I agreed.

Imagine it, if you will. Three middle-aged people stumbling down a dark, deserted road, dressed as chickens, wandering through an environment populated by skunks, the occasional cougar, and other animals known to be sometimes hostile to poultry. We could see nothing. We said nothing. Altona was in heels. After about twenty minutes, she handed her salad to Virgil and climbed wordlessly onto my back. We hiked on.

It began to rain. It began to rain hard. Whatever adhesive Altona had used to attach the feathers to our coveralls and her bustier was water soluble. One by one the feathers fell. We scattered them behind us, like Hansel and Hansel and Gretel. Still, we said nothing. We were very, very wet. At one point, Virgil stumbled, and the Thai salad flew from his hands. Spicy noodles hung all over the underbrush, like tinsel. Altona snuffled.

It was after midnight by the time we reached the hall, cold, saturated, discouraged, and hungry. The party had just peaked. It had been a great success. The food had been wonderful. We knew it had been wonderful because it was all gone. We walked in the door, dripping and featherless, wearing our coveralls and balaclavas and bustier, just in time to see the prize for best costume awarded to a man dressed as a chicken. This was too much for Altona. She began to cry: not a quiet sobbing, but great, heart-wracking bellows. It did rather cast a pall. Things wound down shortly after our conspicuous arrival.

Abel Wackaugh was there, luckily. He gave us all a ride home and stopped long enough to fix the stove.

"Just a fuse, for gosh sakes," he reported.

I made some conciliatory hot chocolate, but Altona declined the offer. She slept in a guest room and left without saying goodbye in the morning. It took her three days to bring herself to speak to me. And then she was silent for another three after a photograph of our dripping, bedraggled entrance into the hall appeared in the *Rumor*. J. MacDonald Bellweather has no sense of decorum, discretion, or loyalty to employees.

"Think I'd pass up an opportunity to print a picture like that?" he asked, when I called to complain on Altona's behalf. "Hell's bells! Funniest thing I've ever seen. Don't you worry about Altona. She'll get over it!"

And he was right. She did. Today, things were as they ought to be. We discussed our plans for a Christmas potluck, and she laughed at my suggestion that I cook the turkey on the manifold. She is coming over this weekend to help us bake our fruitcake. In short, her mood was as sunny as the day. She was especially jovial because she was able to get a candid photograph of her editor, in his kilt, bending over to pick up a dropped quarter.

"Now I know what he wears underneath," she smirked.

The next time Mac goes on vacation, leaving Altona in charge of putting out the paper, you can bet that the whole valley will share that knowledge. I must confess that the four of us snickered at the prospect as we sat on the bench, watching the frolicking dogs: pure, happy souls, not one of whom could even begin to understand the concept of vengeance. ⬆

Kevin

I don't like to speak ill of the dead, but T. S. Eliot handed us a big crock when he called April the cruellest month. That particular rap has to be pinned on November. February comes in a close second. For me, those are the truly bleak times: short days, bad light, lousy weather, no holidays. Blah!

"The blahs" are what I call the condition that settles in round about November time. I think most people—especially those of us who live in northern latitudes—know the blahs, although some may call them by another name. Depression. Malaise. Seasonal Affective Disorder. There's nothing you can do about the blahs. There's no inoculation or other prophylaxis. The only protection against the blahs is to anticipate their arrival and be nice to yourself. Keep some flowers in the house. Buy new towels. Take a weekend away, if you can manage it.

Coming here was a good thing. Kind hosts. A beautiful house. A quiet place. And best of all, a welcoming kitchen. It's my favourite room, the warm heart of a house. It's where I like to sit with friends to dish and have coffee. It's where I always gravitate at parties. It was especially nice to be allowed into your kitchen for the fruitcake session. That made me feel right at home. It's one of my November rituals, too, and one that I have to get to in the next couple of days if I want my cake to be ripe for the big day.

This is the first time I've had the chance to study another method. Your *modus operandi* is not so very different from mine, though of course there are some variations. It was a privilege to be let in on some of the secrets that came down to you through your mother. In my family, the annual construction of a festive fruitcake has always been the province and responsibility of the men. It is part of a patrilineal heritage that has been handed, torchlike, from the sons of one generation unto the next. I've never had any interest in genealogy. But I'd be willing to bet that if I had the patience or the research skills, I could trace the history of the cake back to William the Conqueror, or find its ingredients listed in the Domesday Book.

The recipe I use has been treated like a spell or incantation. It's never been written down, as though transcription would sap it of its strength. It has been passed on orally, from father to son, in much the same way a Bornean bushman might teach his male children how to make a potent poison for an arrow tip or to predict the weather by studying the ponderous ways of the tapir.

I am the youngest of six siblings, and the only boy. My birth was the cause of some celebration: for my mother because it meant that she had at last fulfilled what she seemed to regard as some sort of marital obligation and could finally stop competing with next-door Mrs. Donnely, who in any case was Catholic; and for my father because it meant that the patrilineal means of fruitcake transmission could be preserved.

I can no more remember when I learned to recite the cake's ingredients than I can call to mind the day I learned "Jack be nimble, Jack be quick" or "Thirty days hath September." It was just always there, somehow. When autumn came around, the other little boys, my neighbours, went out with their fathers into the nearby marsh or forest. There, they gunned down ducks or deer. For me, the sure sign of the shifting of the seasons was the Saturday morning early in November when my mother—by way of some prior arrangement—would gather up my sisters and take them shopping, then to lunch in the Paddlewheel Room at the Bay. There they would sit in the section that had been specially cordoned off "For Ladies Only" and order the Denver sandwiches and strawberry milkshakes that had made the place a legend in its own time.

Once the women had gone into temporary purdah, we could begin. Off we went to the supermarket to collect the citron, the spices, the eggs, the flour, the raisins, the dates, the currants, the maraschino cherries, the pecans and almonds. Next, to the liquor store for the brandy. Then, back home and ensconced in our laboratory, we worked quickly and silently at the assemblage, the sorcerer taking great care to supervise and instruct his eager apprentice. Everything was done according to the antique formula. When the batter was finally consigned to the tin that was kept for this specific purpose, the nascent cake was decorated with almonds and cherries that were laid out in an unvarying pattern. We eased the cake into oven and spent the remainder of the afternoon sitting quietly, studying the changing light. At the appointed hour, the cake was withdrawn, allowed to cool, then embalmed in a brandy-soaked cheesecloth and stored in a dark cupboard where it would ripen until Christmas Eve. Then it was exhumed, all moist and redolent, a sweet hymn to the past, a present joy, and a blessing on the future. Each year's new fruitcake signalled that good things endured, that custom persevered, that though the earth might wobble on its axis, still it wound on.

As the only initiate into these ancient rites, I carried a certain burden of responsibility. It was expected that in time's due course I would sire a son to whom I could pass the family secrets. My eventual disclosure that I would *not* be dredging the gene pool all the deeper caused such a rupture and prolonged carry-on that I finally thought it best to pack up my few possessions and beat it to the coast. Which is where I have come to roost.

Five or so years ago, Archie and Leonard and I were sitting around in my kitchen, sifting through the growing rubble of the years, searching for the precise moment we were able to put a name to what it was that made us different from the rest of the boys of our young acquaintance.

"I owe it all to Ed Sullivan," said Archie. "Remember him? We were watching one Sunday night. There were the usual ho-hum circus acts, some oily tenor who was singing at the Met, Topo Gigio. And then—Liberace! He was seated at a white grand piano. I remember that was he all decked out in furs and sequins. He had this immense hair and a kind of predatory mouth. It was set in a kind of 'all the better to eat you with' grin. There was the candelabra, of course. He was playing 'Moon River,' swanning and swooning all over the keyboard. God, he was wonderful! But my brothers didn't think so. They took one look at him and said, 'What a fruitcake!' 'Yeah, what a fruitcake!' I murmured, but without any of their manly heartiness. Or conviction.

"And that was when I figured out which way was north on my compass. I can peg it to that precise moment. I understood then that Liberace and I had something in common. I was what *he* was, and what he was was something no boy would ever want to be. A fruitcake. Dear God, didn't that become a word to choke on! It took a long time before it turned from a point of shame into a badge of honour. Now that I think of it, it's even apt. I've improved with age, and I'm at my best when saturated with alcohol."

Though I chuckled at Archie's arch story, it was all too easy to read the sadness between the lines. It made me think, too. It roused in me a sense of something like responsibility. I had experienced a familial breach; but I had not been stripped of my heritage. I had been entrusted with the fruitcake recipe. It was a sacred charge. A living thing. But confined as it was to the cage of my skull, it could do no earthly good. I had the power—indeed, the obligation—to set it loose in the world. In the absence of an heir, it seemed clear to me that I could do no better than to bestow the essence of the wizardry on these two friends. I had no son. But I could choose these brothers.

I put the plan to my friends, and they quickly agreed. The very next day, we assembled again, and I began the business of transmission and instruction. We made an admirable cake and shared it at Christmas. The next year, we repeated the process. Neither Archie nor Leonard were novices in the kitchen, and both were eager initiates. Though they grumbled a bit at my insistence that, for the sake of tradition, there should be no recourse to a written recipe, and though Archie complained that the years had brought with them a certain intransigence of memory, by the third go-round—by which time a sense of renewed tradition had firmly taken hold—they had both become adept at the procedure. I felt quite sure that with another year's practice they would be fully equipped to go out as fruitcake evangelists, should they feel so inclined.

But for Archie, there wasn't to be another year. The first pneumonia came at Easter. He was dead before the summer was out. He didn't trouble to linger. I guess he was one of the lucky ones. You can appreciate, then, that it was with a certain sense of sadness and nostalgia that Leonard and I met on All Souls' Day to make the fruitcake. We chanted lowly and slowly as we mixed and measured:

Cinnamon, cloves, allspice, nutmeg,
currants, raisins, pecans, almonds,
citron, sugar, fifteen egg yolks lightly beaten,
half a cup of brandy . . .

There is a good deal more brandy in a bottle than can be accommodated by a single fruitcake. Once it was in the oven, we honoured Archie with a second wake. We told stories about him and wept. We recalled his fruitcake story and wept. We told a story he loved to tell and that no one could tell better: an apocryphal story about a visit Liberace paid to Vancouver. According to the story, he had turned up at a down-at-the-heels seafood restaurant called the Only. It's famous, legendary even, because the food is good and it's in a pretty rough section of town. It is not the kind of place you'd expect to see a visiting celebrity. Here's how I remember the gospel according to Archie. He would tell it in the present tense, as if he were watching it happen:

A great stretch limo pulls up to the Only. Liberace emerges in a cloud of scent and wafts inside. The staff is astonished out of their habitual surliness. The pedlars of human flesh and the sad, sad drunks gather in the doorway, gaping. There are longshoremen and social workers with their spoons frozen in midair, between clam chowder and mouth. Liberace perches primly on one of the stools at the U-shaped counter, dressed in an ermine-fringed cape, rings on every finger, his face thick with stage make-up, sequins sparkling like salmon scales. He is a fish out of water, not drowning in the treacherous air but strutting along the pebbled shore, nonchalantly singing "La Donna E Mobile." He is an astonishing fiction, an artist whose grandest creation is himself and who is strong enough in that self to stride into what would normally have been the most hostile of Coliseums, and cow even the most ferocious lion or gladiator.

(When Archie told the story, we would hang on his every word, like children who know full well that the wolf will slide down the chimney into the boiling pot but never tire of hearing it.)

Liberace sits in the thickening silence and studies the menu. No one moves. No one breathes. He closes the menu, replaces it in the little metal rack, smiles that famous smile at the waitress, and says, in his mellifluous and unabashedly fruitcake voice, "Halibut and chips, please." Nothing more remarkable than that. But as soon as the words are out, the whole restaurant erupts into cheers. Drunks and hookers and stevedores stand and stamp their feet and whistle and clap and hoot and carry on. He takes it all as nothing more than his due. He is Liberace, whose whole glittering life has been built by the laying of triumph on triumph.

The family fruitcake takes four hours to bake. By the time it was done, Leonard and I had polished off every intoxicant in the house and had laughed and cried ourselves into a state of near exhaustion. What comes next is the stuff of supermarket tabloids. You can believe it or discard it as you choose. I can only tell you what I swear to be the truth.

When I pulled out the fruitcake from the oven, its aroma of brandy, fruit, and timelessness brought the tears back to my eyes. I looked down at the cake, and saw—very plainly, even through the smudging of weepy nostalgia—the face of Liberace. His portrait had been baked onto the top of the cake: the sweep of hair, the dimpled chin, the grin, the teeth. There was no mistaking it. I gaped, just as the longshoremen must have done all those years ago in the Only. My chin touched my chest. I gurgled. I gasped. And I howled! I tossed the fruitcake into the air. It spun about and landed, face downward, on the kitchen linoleum.

Leonard came running—staggering, rather—from the living room. It was fully five minutes before I could sputter out the story. He picked the cake up off the floor. It was altogether squashed. The decorative arrangement of almonds and cherries was no more. And, of course, there was no Liberace.

"But he was there," I said. "Plain as day."

There was a long silence while Leonard searched for something neutral to say. Then, from the living room, we heard the thin sound of a toy piano: the first few bars of "Moon River."

We hurried to investigate and found the room as we had left it, save for one thing. I have a Christmas cactus. I grew it from a cutting I took from my parents' home. Like the fruitcake recipe, it has been in the family for generations. I have treated it tenderly over the years, and it has grown to an impressive size. It is admirable for the regularity of its habits. The buds appear early in November, and the blossoms are in place by the third Sunday of Advent.

Leonard and I have talked about it since and wondered who engineered the little miracle. Liberace? Archie? Or the two working in tandem? All that we know for sure is this. Every stem of the cactus had flowered, in the twinkling of an eye. It was the most beautiful thing I have ever seen. It looked just like a candelabra spilling fuchsia flames.

And that's my really truly story. I can hardly credit it myself. But that was one November that I walked around in a state of prolonged wonderment. The blahs didn't stand a chance.

Thanks again for a lovely time. Perhaps we can arrange to exchange slices of fruitcake around Christmas time. As Simple Simon said, I'd love to taste your wares. I'm sure you turn out a very fine product. But you'd have to go a long way to make something that's better than mine! ♠

Envoi

Way back in the fifties, in the dim dark days when we spoke of Fahrenheit, quarts, and miles, Abel Wackaugh was visited by the notion that he should have some kind of promotional device for his newly established hardware store *cum* barber shop. He wanted a geegaw he might bestow upon regular customers; a trifle they could carry away as a souvenir of their haircut (as though the haircut were not souvenir enough!); a *chachka* they might pack off with their washers, drill bits, and screws. It was his intention, of course, that the clientele upon whom he smiled would accord this little bibelot a place of honour in their homes or offices, where it would be admired by their visitors. This, thought Abel, would be a subtle and graceful way of spreading the word about his rather unique operation. For where else could you get a shave and a haircut and have your axe sharpened at the same time?

He considered all the usual tokens: pens, ashtrays, calendars, placemats, and so on. But these were far too pedestrian. I have a hazy recollection of visiting his store with Mother and hearing him go on at some length about how challenging it was proving to settle on just the right item to serve his purposes. She suggested a line of walking sticks might be just the thing.

"Walking sticks?"

"As in cane and Abel," Mother deadpanned. I'm not entirely sure he got it.

That would have been forty years ago, or more. Abel had only recently come to the valley and was living in rather rustic circumstances, renting a tiny cabin that was uncluttered by such amenities as insulation. The only heat source was a sad and anaemic wood stove. One especially chilly morning, Abel stood squinting at himself before his breath-misted mirror, shaving as best he could and pondering the while what the temperature might be in his frosty little hut.

It is at times just such as these that inspiration is inclined to leave a calling card. In a moment of startling clarity, Abel hit upon the idea of designing a self-commemorating shaving mirror that would also serve as a thermometer. It was such a brilliant stroke, and so perfectly suited for a dual-purpose business such as his own, that he sat down that very morning and designed just such a thing. It was a cunning piece of craftsmanship: the actual mirror mounted on wood, with the thermometer attached to the left flank of the glass. In the bottom right was a black silhouette of a spindly birch tree, with a stag and doe grazing beneath. Emblazoned across the top of the mirror, in an impressive but almost indecipherable gothic script, were the words "ABEL WACKAUGH HARDWARE AND BAR-BERING." These were small mirrors, and with the inclusion of the thermometer and various bits of artwork and text that festooned the working surface, there was not a great deal of space available in which to view one's face.

Abel, however, was thrilled with the product and showed great largesse in making them available to his clients and cronies, who received them with polite puzzlement. While Abel's conviction that everyone should have access to intelligence about the temperature while shaving was admirable, it was not a concern that was generally shared by other valley dwellers, most of whom had bathrooms that were moderately warm.

The mirrors, though widely distributed, were not for the most part hung in their intended places. Most were consigned to the bottom drawer of a dresser and forgotten about until someone was seized by a tidy fit and thought to send it to the church for the annual Christmas jumble sale. They still turn up there, although rather more rarely now.

Mother liked Abel and wanted to do the right thing by his offering. She couldn't feature it in the bathroom (and at that time, neither Hector nor I had started to shave), so she hung it on the inside of the door of the utility cupboard. And there it remained, keeping company with extension cords, fuses, and disused mops and brooms. It had no purpose, other than to remind whomever was opening the closet who they were and to register the very consistent temperature of 72 degrees.

This summer, however, the thermometer that had hung outside the kitchen window for the last dozen or so years was broken when it was knocked from its fastenings by an errant tennis ball. We never got around to replacing it, and in fact I have never much missed it until tonight. Tonight, because the weather has gone all haywire, I have an abiding need to be able to measure the outside temperature. And so, to this end, I have taken Abel's mirror from the nail on which it has hung so long and placed it on the back porch. I expected it would prove little more than a fossil; that the mercury wouldn't budge a jot from its habitual comfort zone. But within a very few moments, it kicked into action and began to plunge. When last I checked, it was reporting a temperature of 18 degrees Fahrenheit, which is very cool for these parts. And it seems that it might get chillier still.

It was two nights ago that this severe and atypical cold spell skied over the hills and into our little valley. I woke at 4 A.M., for no apparent reason, but with the firm conviction that I had heard something: a great cracking sound, as though the world had seized up on its axis.

All that day, the phone lines hummed with the meteorological musings of our friends and neighbours. We just couldn't get enough of calling one another up to talk about the weather. It was as if we required the report of someone else's experience to believe that our meek and mild-mannered temperature could stoop so low. Amazed weathermen would come on the radio to tell us what we already knew: that it was damn chilly and likely to stay that way for some time.

Then, all at once, the radios ceased their chatter. For miles around, fridges and electric clocks and hot water heaters shuddered, sighed, and slept. All up and down the valley, people walked about their houses, flicking light switches and staring hopefully and rather stupidly at their dormant lamps, waiting for something to happen. It was all for naught. The electricity had simply tired of being taken so much for granted. It had decided it would flow no more. This is how it has been for over twenty-four hours.

Happily, we are taking our annual breather from the business of filling beds and cooking breakfasts. I would feel very sorry for any guest who had taken the time to come to this out-of-the-way place and then had to put up with the rather primitive conditions that have been foisted on us by circumstance. This power outage has proved a considerable inconvenience for everyone, although there is a certain sense of adventure in the air, too. All the perishables have been moved into the amply refrigerated great outdoors and secured against the intrusions of whatever fauna might be brave enough to be out and about. Up and down the valley, the old and infirm have been wrested from their roosts, wrapped in afghans, and propped up by their neighbours' stoves. Kerosene lamps and candles have come into their own.

I am writing this in the library, by the flickering glow of the fire—now our only source of heat—and by the supplementary light of three candles. These I have placed in three wine bottles, one of which I had to empty before I could use it. Waffle is staring into the fire, in her mystic way. Mrs. Rochester, who miraculously uttered not a single word of protest or blasphemy when I moved her from the too cold kitchen, is asleep in her covered cage, her head tucked beneath a wing. With the exception of these two familiars, I am alone in the house, which is a rare enough occurrence. Hector and Altona are keeping one another warm at her place; and tomorrow, they are leaving on a four-day driving trip to Oregon. Hector has never seen the dunes on that coast (nor have I, come to that); and Altona thinks that she might like to set her next novel there.

"It's perfect!" she told me the other night. "Sea and sand and wild, wild winds! Just the place for high romance."

"Have you got a plot in mind?" I asked.

"Sure! It's bad luck to give too much away before you're out of the woods, but I'll tell you this much. It has to do with a beautiful young woman, an accountant, who goes to work at this hotel run by a confirmed bachelor. He loves her. She loves him. They want to give themselves to each other, wholly and without reserve. But there's something—or someone—that stands in their way."

"Ah. A relative, perhaps?"

"Could be. You'll just have to wait and see."

"I'm on pins and needles already," I said, and kissed her on the cheek in a brotherly fashion.

Anyone who does not know Altona and overheard this exchange may have thought he detected an undercurrent of irony or thinly veiled bitterness in those words. Schooled as we are in the conventions of potboiler romance, it is natural enough to suppose that Altona must regard me—and the bed and breakfast—as stumbling blocks in the way of her own proprietary interests vis-à-vis Hector. According to the well-known formula, she would eventually stage a "him or me" scene, in which she would assert emotional primacy and stake her unique claim to my brother's affections and devotion. This is the sort of incident that might very well unravel in one of her novels. But Altona does not live by fiction, and her life does not mimic her art.

I suppose that when Hector and Altona first forged their bond, I half expected they would decide to set up shop together. I would be a liar if I said that I didn't look on that prospect with some sense of trepidation. After all these years of sharing a house with my twin, and with all the habits and unspoken dependencies that accrue over a lifetime of cohabitation, I could hardly pretend that I welcomed the looming spectre of significant change. On the other hand, I need scarcely say that if Hector were to decide that his best shot at happiness lay elsewhere and chose to leave this place, I would wish him good luck and godspeed. We have never taken a vow that binds us one to another or to our status as bachelors. But Hector has shown no inclination to radically shift gears and start afresh; and happily, Altona seems not at all keen on pressuring him to change his circumstances in the slightest. We have never discussed, in any straightforward way, the dynamics of our household and her role in it. Whatever understandings we have come to about blood and water have been reached tacitly. Her wry little remark about the plot of her new romance is as close as she has come with me to any overt airing of the mechanics of our tripartite arrangement.

I can't imagine that Altona has any interest in disturbing the status quo. She likes having both her independence and the certainty of good company and easy affection. She has never given any sign of being overly possessive, and I think I can safely say that she loves Hector for who he is; and as I am a part of his world, she simply folds me into the mix and loves me too in her all-inclusive way. It makes me happy to see them. They are two people who are well matched, whose needs and present circumstances mesh without grinding. And that is a rare and lovely thing in this world.

I do not often take the time to look long and hard at myself and wonder at the whys and wherefores of my own long celibacy. It is not as though I have never been in love. I have, once or twice. It was pleasantly electric. A good way of feeling alive. And there have been times when I've regretted that I've never found someone who at first excited concupiscent longing and then went on to become an enduring, intimate companion. Some years ago, when I was going through what I guess must have been a sort of mid-life crisis, I felt deeply oppressed by the relentless march of irretrievable time. I saw a life of solitary sameness stretching before me and came close to choking on the gnawing desperation of loneliness. It was a bad patch. It was surely not coincidental that it was during this period that I had my heart attack. Could there be a more telling or appropriate physical acting out of a psychic malaise? But I came though it: intact and, relatively speaking, happy.

Almost an hour has passed since I wrote those last words. I set down my pen, and went out to the back porch to check on the temperature. Fourteen degrees Fahrenheit, according to the thermometer that lay dormant all those years but has been now jarred into a rude awakening. I exhaled warm breath on the mirror, and it misted immediately. On cold days, when we were children, Hector and I would blow on the window of our room and write our names in the beady condensation. Little people the world over must do the same: leave their names as a tangible trace on windows, in sand, on tree bark. An inscription of selfhood: this is me, and I passed here. I drew a big question mark on Abel's mirror, set it back down on the porch, and went up to my room to retrieve yet another sweater. Now, my natural defences are bolstered by five pullovers and an oversized cardigan, all of them squaring off against the invasive cold. I look quite a lot like the Michelin man.

Waffle followed me on my mission, trotting along behind like a loyal dog. This is not her usual way. I take her anomalous display of companionability as a demonstration that she, too, shares a sense of wonderment at what we seem to have come to, here in our valley. Man and cat together, we followed the flashlight's narrow beacon up the familiar stairs and down the hallway. I opened every door, feeling my breath catch ever so slightly in my throat at each turn of the handle: another emotional remnant of childhood, when every ostensibly empty room might well house an unimagined horror. But the light, peeling back small strips of concealing darkness from the hulking forms of the beds, tables, washstands, and bookcases, revealed that everything was as it ought to be. I got the sweater from my room—the same room I have slept in all my life—and continued up the narrow flight at the end of the hall that leads to the attic.

Our attic is a cupola room, with windows on all sides. There is a telescope there that belonged to our grandfather. It is a brass instrument, more decorative than functional, but not without some power to magnify. It is mounted on a stand that rotates 180 degrees. You can fix your eye to the scope, do a slow revolve, and take in the whole of the valley. Or you can tip it up and survey the stars. As Waffle wound about my ankles, I squinted through the old lens at the night sky. It was shockingly clear.

Mother used to try to teach us the names of the constellations.

"That's Orion. Look for the belt."

"There's the Big Dipper. See how much like a dipper it looks?"

"Look! Cassiopeia's chair!"

But I was hopeless. I could never find the pictures. All I could see was a random scattering of dots, and no amount of peering at the sky would make them form themselves into a recognizable image.

Some things never change. I looked through the telescope again and saw only a crazy array and spill of pinpoints of light. None of it made sense. I looked down and around the valley, illuminated only by the stars and an ambitious half-moon. I could see smoke rising from chimneys. But, of course, there were no lamps to punctuate the dark. Nothing stirred.

It was so quiet! I half-believed that I was the last one left breathing on the earth. I am partial to solitude, it's true. But the idea of being the only one extant was not one I warmed to. So to prove myself wrong, I stood in the middle of the attic and listened to the sounds that make up what we call silence. I heard Waffle's soft purr as she sat looking through the window. I heard the creaking of the settling house. I listened deeper. I heard the warble of the candles two storeys down, heard the frost thicken on the windowpane, heard a frog stir in the mud at the bottom of a paralysed pond.

And then—something different, something infinitely more distant and more real. A delicate, feathery hum. It was so faint and so high! It balanced right on the cusp of my hearing. I strained to listen closer. I scrunched up my eyes and pushed hard against the inside of my ears. I listened as intently and as deeply as I could. But it was gone. Somehow, in that overexertion of the sense, I had scrambled whatever channel I had stumbled on.

What was it, I wonder? It had been, in the truest sense of the word, ethereal. Otherworldly. Was it the pure, wordless singing of the cold? The music of the spheres? Out loud, I said the words, "A multitude of the heavenly host." Who can say? If such things are possible, then they surely transpire on nights like tonight, with a sky such as this.

I left the attic, closed the door, and came back to the library. All these books, side by side. I could release a clamour of voices just by opening any one of their covers. But this is not a night meant for company, however genial and familiar. I've added a log to the dwindling fire. This will be the last one tonight to suffer the hot love of the flames. Their crackle is gleeful and rapacious. They roar their approval. It's an unsettling sight. But they will be done, soon enough. And when they are finished their devouring, the restful silence will return. The only sounds will be the scratching of my pen on this paper and the slight coughing of these three candles, these three dwindling magi, each one carrying a gift of gold, each small light shining as the earth rockets through space, spinning away from the year's darkest day, spinning towards a new year when anything might happen, and everything most assuredly will. ♠